TURBO JETSLAMS

Proof #29
of the
Non-Existence of God

Also by Jass Richards

(Rev and Dylan series)

License to Do That

The Blasphemy Tour

The Road Trip Dialogues

(Brett series)

Dogs Just Wanna Have Fun

This Will Not Look Good on My Resume

Turbo Jetslams

Proof #29
of the
Non-Existence of God

Jass Richards

Magenta

Published by Magenta

Magenta

TurboJetslams: Proof #29 of the Non-Existence of God

ISBN 978-1-926891-65-1

Cover design by Jass Richards
Formatting and interior book design by Elizabeth Beeton

www.jassrichards.com

I would like to acknowledge funding support from the Ontario Arts Council, an agency of the Government of Ontario.

ONTARIO ARTS COUNCIL
CONSEIL DES ARTS DE L'ONTARIO

an Ontario government agency
un organisme du gouvernement de l'Ontario

Library and Archives Canada Cataloguing in Publication

Richards, Jass, author
TurboJetslams : proof #29 of the non-existence of God / Jass Richards.

Issued in print and electronic formats.
ISBN 978-1-926891-65-1 (paperback).--ISBN 978-1-926891-66-8 (html).--
ISBN 978-1-926891-67-5 (pdf)

I. Title.

PS8635.I268T87 2016 C813'.6 C2015-904272-0
C2015-904273-9

This is a work of fiction.

But any resemblance to real persons,
living or deceased,
is completely justified.

All her life, she'd wanted to live in a cabin on a lake in a forest.

And do nothing but read, write, and think.

After ten years of crappy, part-time, occasional, relief, and temp jobs, two years of which were spent counting cars at busy intersections—what else does one do with degrees in Literature, Psychology, and Philosophy?—she managed to have $10,000 in her savings account. Enough for a down payment. So she started calling real estate agents a little north of Toronto.

When she told them what she wanted and what she could afford, they laughed.

So she called real estate agents a bit further north. They still laughed, but not as loudly.

She kept calling, further and further north, until finally one agent, just this side of the Arctic circle, simply asked, "How soon do you need it?"

"No rush," Vic replied. "I'll just keep renting until I find the perfect spot."

Several months and a few near-perfect spots later, the agent took her to a cabin for sale on Paradise Lake.

She started falling in love with the place on the drive in. They'd driven ten miles from the nearest town, five miles on dirt roads, the last two of which wound through trees on either side.

She continued to fall in love as they turned into the driveway. It was long. You couldn't even see the cabin from the road.

And as soon as she walked around to the lake side, she knew.

It was perfect.

"Yes," she said. "I'll take it."

The agent stared at her. "Don't you want to see the inside?"

"Okay." But it didn't really matter. The washroom could have required some assembly. The floor could have been missing. She didn't care. Because she couldn't take her eyes off the view.

The lake was surrounded by hills, all heavily treed, all wilder-nessey.

The cabin was on the side of a small cove at the end of the lake. Crown land curved around the cove, extending into a pen-insula across from the cabin. So she saw nothing but water and trees, lake and forest.

She felt like a violin that had finally found its bow.

There was a vacant lot on the right. Again, heavily treed and wildernessey.

"It belongs to the gentleman two cottages down," the agent said. "I think he's keeping it for his kids."

"Well, if he ever wants to sell it, tell him I'll buy it," she told her. "In a heartbeat."

As she stood there, unwilling, un*able* to move, looking out at the little cove, the water, the trees rising all around, it felt...right. Just—right.

After nineteen addresses in ten years, she was home.

The lake side of the lot was a bit steep, but it was certainly do-able. Maybe when she was sixty and had no knees left, she'd have to put in stairs, ramps, or a pulley system, but for now, it was good. She simply made a little twisty path between the trees, saplings, weeds, and whatever.

There was no point in cutting, clearing, and planting grass. The slope she was on would probably erode away if she so much as touched it, and in any case, it would be impossible to mow. Not that she had a lawnmower. Or intended to get one.

So she left it all, front and back, as is. Better for the bugs that way. As she found out the following spring.

She spent the first two months, September and October, making it habitable. All of the bits in the washroom *were* assembled, and there *was* a floor, but...

She got rid of the cookstove that was in the middle of the living room slash kitchen and took out the counter that divided the space in two. She wanted room to dance.

Next, she replaced the huge fridge with a smaller one. Got rid of the oven and put in a doggy door. Put a mattress in the corner at the back. Took out the wall between the two small bedrooms. Almost took out the supporting beam. (She was having such fun with the sledgehammer.)

Good thing her new neighbours, an elderly couple living at the other end of the lane, happened to come by. (She discovered, much to her delight, that there were only three others living on the lake: in addition to the elderly Johnsons, there was MaryAnn, who lived across the lake and had two young boys, and the Campbells, who lived just past the Johnsons and were expecting their first child. There were also three houses on top of the hill coming in, all occupied by retirees. There were a few summer cottages, whose owners may have been up every now and then through the fall; their presence wasn't particularly noteworthy.)

She also took out the doors and closets of the two small bedrooms. Ex-bedrooms. Used the wood to build bookshelves onto three of the walls, put her desk against the fourth—the one with the large window, overlooking the lake—and had herself a study.

Then she cleaned the place. The soot on the walls was so thick from the cookstove that she had to change the water in her pail every five minutes. She washed, rinsed, washed, and rinsed *everything*.

She spent the next two months, November and December, understanding what the word 'winterized' meant. Or, rather, what it didn't mean.

And then she spent the next fifteen years making her cabin on a lake in a forest even better. She had a trench dug for the water line to the lake, but even so, had to dive into ice cold water three springs in a row to fix the foot valve, having been without running water for half the winter: one January, the valve sunk to the bottom and got stuck in the muck; the next year, it rose to the top and froze into the ice; the third year—she couldn't remember what happened to it the third year. She did remember that when she was ten feet under and taking too long, she reached such a oneness with the world, she was convinced she could breathe water. After all, it had oxygen in it, right? $H_2\mathit{O}$.

It would take another ten years before she was able to afford a well, but she hadn't drowned in the interim, so that was okay. In the meantime, there was a delightful spring on the adjacent crown land, and it was all very Henry David Thoreau to haul water. For the first two weeks.

She tarred the leaking shingled roof every few months, apparently never tarring the actual holes, until she could afford a metal roof.

She replaced the windows one at a time, as she could afford them, with glazed double-paned sliders. And eventually folded up for good the plastic she'd been putting over them every winter.

She had huge eight-by-eight picture windows put in the main room on either side of the fireplace. Going with all-glass, no crossbars or divisions for inserted screened windows at the top or bottom, turned out to be a bit of a ventilation mistake, but oh, the view! She put her couch—once she discovered laptops, she started writing not while seated at her desk but while sunk into the couch (which had been given to her by one of her piano students, probably only because that was easier than carting it to the dump—it had a broken spring, hence the 'sunk')—in front of one of the large windows, angling it just so, to see the sun sparkle on the water through the gaps among the trees…

Speaking of the fireplace, she discovered that despite the implicit presence of fire, a fireplace is not a source of heat. If you just stand in front of it, your hands might get warm. Provided you shove them into the flames. But otherwise? And since she'd cleverly had the baseboard heater removed—it ruined the aesthetics, being under just one of the glorious pair of picture windows—she was very cold the first winter. She bought a woodstove for the second winter. A Canadian Tire special. It was all she could afford. But three years later, she got a high-quality Regency fireplace insert. Much neater than the woodstove jutting out in the way of her dancing. But then, since she couldn't see the pretty flames from her couch in the evenings, she replaced it the following year with an Osborne insert, the one with the bay window door. Eventually, since heat doesn't travel sideways, she bought a furnace. And so, after fifteen years, she was finally *warm*.

She replaced the Picasso-wannabe dock with a dockraft: an eight by eight raft that doubled as a dock. It had one end anchored solidly on shore, the other end floating on barrels, which meant she didn't have to haul it out every winter—not that she could have done that, given the vertical—because it could just rise and fall with the ice, instead of getting yanked apart by it.

Blackflies swarm, she discovered, and they crawl on your arms, and on your legs, and along your hair line, and in your ears, and your eyes, and your nose— And they bite. Blackflies are near-microscopic piranhas with wings. This—this swarming and crawling and biting—goes on for a good six weeks. In mid-April, if it was warm enough, she could finally go outside after the long winter, but a mere four weeks later, in mid-May, the blackflies drove her back in. Between the blackflies and the mosquitos (and the deer flies and the horse flies), once she swatted at herself so hard, she knocked herself out. So as soon as blackfly season ended, and she'd recovered consciousness, she built a screened-in gazebo. (No frickin' way she was going to build it *during* blackfly season.)

(She also discovered, by the way, how impossible it is to get a roof on if you make it first, on the ground. Even if you have your elderly neighbours to help.)

Alas, the gazebo didn't keep the bugs out, and for the life of her she couldn't figure out why. So a few years later, she had a screened porch added to the cabin. When the guy moved the gazebo, because it was exactly where the porch was going to go, he ended up setting it in a slightly depressed area behind the cabin, and she could see, clear as the daylight coming through, a space all along the top. She bought a caulking gun and went crazy. Good to have a back-up.

Once the screened-in porch was done, she was delighted to discover that when she was in it, she could hear the spring gurgling up. So she carefully arranged the rocks just so, for the falling water to make the prettiest tinkly sound.

(One of the summer people used the spring for water and always tossed aside her carefully arranged rocks—did he think nature had arranged them just so? She finally asked him if he could just *set* them aside, sensing that it would be going too far to ask him to please just put them back the way he found them. Why? he asked belligerently. She told him. Politely. He looked at her like she was kidding, no doubt unable to take a woman seriously. And kept tossing the rocks into the bush.)

She also had the cabin extended a bit, while she as at it, so she could move her bed to the lake side. She had a window put in right above it so at night, she could hear the beautiful calls of the loons.

She replaced the narrow lakeside porch—one day she stepped out the door and it just sort of swooned to the left and settled onto the ground with a sigh—with a sturdy deck, large enough for a lounge chair, a tree trunk table on the left for her work, and another on the right for her tea.

And, finally, she took advantage of a government program that would subsidize adding more insulation to her cabin (all it had was eight inches of that pink stuff) (which had, in the crawlspace, fallen down, and she spent a day in hell, strapping it back up so the floor would be warmish). She'd postponed the extra insulation for so long because she thought it had to be added from the inside. Adding it to the outside, to the cabin as it was, just meant adding another layer of siding—instead of dismantling three walls of books in the study and another wall of LPs and CDs in the main space, as well as the kitchen sink, counter, and cupboards.)

Much of this she did by herself. All the while staring at the lake. (Which may account for the numerous injuries she sustained.) (Though the lack of tools, skill, and knowledge may also have played a role.) She couldn't take her eyes off of it. The lake. She still couldn't fifteen years later. Still, fifteen years later, whenever she walked through her cabin, she looked out the large window at her desk, out the sliding glass doors, out the two large windows in the main space—to the water, to the trees, to the nothing but lake and forest.

She found employment, barely, taking whatever she could get, determined to do whatever she had to, to keep her little cabin. She did some freelance editing, some relief work at a women's shelter, some supply teaching. She deejayed for weddings. Scrubbed toilets for minimum wage.

And spent her free time, such as it was, down at the water, on her dockraft, sitting in an old lounge chair, reading, writing, and thinking, Shiggles lying beside her in the sun or underneath her in the shade.

She and Shiggles would watch the ducks come in for a landing, and the heron, who would regularly come to their end of the lake to fish. There was an otter, who wintered one year under her kayak. And of course the loons. In spring, she'd see them, baby on board. And she'd hear them. Oh, the sound. It was absolutely breath-taking.

Sometimes the water was placid beyond belief, and sometimes it was corrugated by the wind. So sometimes the lake would sparkle in the sun, and sometimes it would glitter. She loved the clarity of sparkles when they were distinct and close, but she also loved the distant multitude of them.

And every day between five and six o'clock, when the sun descended to just the right point, its beams at just the right angle, it would light up the trees like a spotlight, then leave them in shadow as it moved in a slow pan from left to right. In spring when the leaves were new, the cove would be transformed into a shimmering chartreuse emerald.

Then for a few minutes, it would stream through the trees, like through cathedral windows, and then a few minutes after that, it would light just the outer tips of the branches, frosting on a cake.

And then it would be dusk.

Often she would sit down on the dockraft at night, listening for the loons and watching the moonlight on the dark water. It had such a different quality from the sunlight, it was a silver gleaming mercury.

The lake was small, a little over a kilometer in length, four hundred meters across at its widest. It took less than an hour to kayak the perimeter, but there was a little creek feeding it, which was delightfully kayakable up to the shallow spot at which point you could just turn around or get out and pull your kayak across the rocks and rapids for a hundred meters and then carry on. And at the end of the lake, which was actually just the swollen end of a river, you could keep going, up the river, for about five miles to the other end where it opened up again into another lake. This is what they did, she and Shiggles. Almost every day. They'd see not just the forementioned ducks, herons, otter, and loons, but also muskrat and the occasional mink. And, as occasionally, deer, moose, and bear, on shore or swimming across.

Sometimes there was just enough wind on the water to make trillions of teeny bubbles that caught the light and swirled amid the showier sparkles, and if she timed it right, in terms of her direction in relation to the sun, it was like paddling into the

Milky Way.

She couldn't see the sun set from her cabin, so she often kayaked back late. If she paddled backwards, she could watch it, sometimes gorgeous orange and red. And then she'd turn around and paddle home in the moonlight, in the starlight, the beavers circling, strong and stealthy, then suddenly swishing and slapping. And the loons calling...

Up the hill about five hundred meters from her cabin, there was an old logging road which led into the forest. They walked and ran for miles. It was amazing. The road, such as it was, crossed over a little babbling brook and then passed a couple small lakes. Several trails split off, going to other small lakes. Her elderly neighbours urged her to buy some pepper spray in case she met a bear, but she didn't think she needed it. She trusted the wildlife to be reasonable. She found a magical spot about five miles in, full of maple trees. In the spring, it was a luminescence of lime and tennis ball green. In the fall, it was a palace of scarlet, gold, and tangerine.

After twelve years of whatever work she could get, she got lucky and landed a few courses at the university an hour away. She continued to live at poverty level, putting the rest of her income toward the mortgage, and three years later had paid it off.

Just in time, because she lost the courses. (She didn't realize that student expectations had risen; they now expected an A merely for showing up.) But by then, high speed internet was finally available at Paradise Lake, and she discovered the wonderful world of online teaching. With no mortgage to pay, her living expenses were cut in half, and given the per course pay of online teaching, she could support herself with just ten hours a week. Sweet.

So she thought she'd write a book. To that point, she'd been writing short pieces—poetry, prose, op-eds, articles. But now, she thought, a book. Yes. Something to do with applied ethics. Maybe a primer for adults. Two of the courses she'd taught at the university were Business Ethics and Contemporary Moral Issues, and it was clear (*quite* clear) that the students thought they already knew right from wrong. After all, it's something we're taught as children.

But most people, she'd observed, hadn't updated their childhood. So ethically speaking, most people remained unsophisticated. Ethically-arrested. Morally-challenged. 'Don't kill', and for the women, the somewhat higher standard, 'Be nice', are woefully inadequate. And 'Do what your parents tell you' is fine until you realize that your parents don't have a clue most of the time. Yes, she thought, I'll write a book about doing the right thing.

No job to go to meant she didn't have to set her alarm. So she just got up when she woke up, and was down at the water by ten, which was when the sun crested the trees and set the cove a-sparkle. She worked—reading, writing, and thinking—for a couple hours, staring at the water, and when she was ready for a break, she and Shiggles went for a long walk in the forest, solutions to the problems, gaps, and rough spots of the morning's work presenting themselves at miles two, three, four.

When they got back, she'd write again, articulating and polishing those solutions, gaps, and rough spots. Then, unless it was one of her two teaching days, they'd go out onto the lake in her kayak until dark.

She spent a week like that. A whole week. The first week, she thought with such deep satisfaction, as she sat in her chair watching the wind blow a patch of sparkles across the water, thinking that the last twenty-five years had been hard, very hard, but worth it—to have gotten her to where she was now, sitting down at the water at her cabin on a lake in a forest, able to do almost nothing but read, write, and think— The first week, she thought, of the rest of my life...

And then one of those TurboJetslams* screamed into the cove.

When it became clear that it wasn't leaving until it had churned and cross-churned every square inch of water, like a dog lifting its leg at every single tree, and she had run out of new and creative ways to express herself, despite the impossibility of being heard above what was unquestionably the most annoying sound on the planet, she packed up her books and her writing pad, and, trying not to breathe, a headache from the fumes already forming, headed back up to her cabin.

And she knew right then and there that Sartre was right.

Absolutely, unequivocally right.

---

* Using any one of the more familiar terms would attract a lawsuit, and 'personal watercraft' sounds just so...inoffensive.

Turned out it was the visiting nephew of the guy who owned one of the cottages across the lake. She sighed with relief. It was a temporary thing then.

The week after the nephew, and the TurboJetslam left, she started hearing another noise. Distant banging and clanging and mechanical groaning and shrieking… She went to investigate.

And found Tim or Lyle, one of MaryAnn's two boys, now both in their mid-twenties, doing some work on their road. What she was hearing was the backhoe Tim or Lyle was on, which she assumed they'd rented for a day.

Or, since whatever they were doing to the road took all day and then some, had rented for a week.

Or two. Because next, they landscaped the entrance, putting huge boulders on either side.

Or three. They rearranged the boulders.

Or four. They widened the trail that led off their driveway up into the hills. Making the dirt bike trail wide enough for ATVs maybe.

Or five. They knocked down the boulders and dragged them half way up the trail.

Then she heard that they weren't renting the backhoe. They'd bought it.

They'd gotten dirt bikes several years ago, when they were maybe fourteen or fifteen. She'd often hear them, zooming from their place, onto the road, then into the bush via the logging road at the top of the hill, unnecessarily shifting gears and revving the engines all the way.

And now they had their very own backhoe. Delightful.

It must've been cheap. Because they weren't, as far as she knew, employed. It looked like something from the 1950s. You could hear it rattling apart as it rolled along.

And when it started digging? Under about two inches of top soil, the whole area was pretty much rock. So when the boys—men—boys—started excavating, it was like nails scraping along a blackboard. Times a hundred. Amplified. Because of the acoustics of the place: small body of water surrounded by forested hills, remember? So imagine a cave. Now put a pool of water in it. An almost-always calm pool of water. Now stand on one side of the pool while someone on the other side drags a huge metal bucket across the rock. For five hours.

Week six, she didn't know what they were doing. But she thought surely it would at some point stop. When the job was done. Right?

Turns out it continued off and on all frickin' summer. Clanging, clattering, crashing, dragging, scraping. All frickin' summer.

Turns out they were making a road through the forest along their side of the lake. Using the brute force of a backhoe apparently.

Until now, the road had gone just as far as their place. Once it joined with the logging road in the forest on this side, she realized, they'd have a racetrack around the lake for their dirt bikes. The ones with the modified mufflers.

Modified? Removed.

Thing is, she never knew which days they'd be at it. With the backhoe. Well, same goes for the dirt bikes, but that was another story.

And she never knew what time. Sometimes she'd be woken up at eight o'clock in the morning by the banging and booming— She once dated a guy who prided himself on being able to pick up a dime with his backhoe; these boys couldn't pick up a dirt bike. Not in ten tries.

Other times, they'd still be at it, or get to it, at eleven o'clock at night. Apparently backhoes have headlights.

And that was another thing. When it started, she had no idea whether it would last for ten minutes (one of the boys must've had ADHD) or ten hours (the other must've had OCD).

And that's basically the definition of torture. Not knowing when the pain will start or how long it will last...

The following summer they were at it again. Possibly pushing the rocks they'd excavated back in to where they had been, so they could drag them out all over again. She could take no more. So she called to inquire.

"Just another day," Lyle said. "Then we're doin' the footings for Don's garage."

"And how long will that take?"

"Oh, most of the week."

"So you're saying that what I heard today, it'll be like that for most of next week, all day, every day?"

"Pretty much."

"Okay, thanks."

She booked a house on Manitoulin Island. She'd always wanted to go. Now seemed as good a time as any. She couldn't really afford the $900, but she couldn't afford to spend the rest of her life in prison on murder charges either.

So she packed up Shiggles, her laptop, some books, some clothes, and left.

She didn't know Manitoulin Island had a lot of skunks. Shiggles found one first day.

It also had porcupines. She found one of those the second day.

And poison ivy? Third day.

The drive back at the end of the week was a long nine hours, including a stop at a drugmart. She'd run out of calamine lotion.

She got home late Saturday night. By the time she unloaded, unpacked, and showered (no soap, that just spreads the rash) (she'd found that out on the fourth day), it was two a.m.

Six hours later, an explosive boom woke her up. What the—wait a minute. She knew that sound. It was the sound of Lyle's excavator bucket being dropped onto rock. Agonizing scraping followed. And then cursing, weeping, and wailing. That was her.

It stopped around eleven. Lunch time?

She called.

"Yeah, we didn't git to 'er last week. We're doin' 'er now."

She was speechless. And not because of the 'doin' 'er'.

So she bought a pair of ear protectors. The kind worn by guys who operate jackhammers.

They did nothing to block the sound of Lyle operating—and she used the word loosely—his backhoe.

So she bought an expensive pair of noise cancelling headphones.

They did nothing to block the sound of Lyle operating—and she used the word wincing—his backhoe.

Then she bought a pair of earplugs, ones with a noise reduction rating of 33. The highest possible.

They did nothing to block the sound of Lyle operating—and she used the word breaking into a sweat—his backhoe.

Then she bought twenty different kinds of earplugs: wax, foam, silicone, rubber, plastic; swimmers', musicians', machine operators'; disposable, reusable.

She figured out that what was most effective was to roll the reusable putty-like kind and stick them deep into her ear canals (carefully following the 'Do Not' instructions on the package).

Unfortunately, the best brand of reusable putty-like earplugs had been discontinued. But she found a store in the UK (ya gotta love eBay) that had 20 boxes left, 8 pairs per box. She bought 'em all.

Even so, she could hear the agonizing shriek of metal on rock, the booming of metal onto rock, the—

She bought a pair of over-the-ear headphones and a portable CD player. She put her earplugs in, put the headphones on, and set the volume on the CD player to max. There, she sighed. That did it.

The following summer, apparently the boys couldn't pay their hydro bill so they used a gas generator. She damn near went insane. It was an old generator. (Of course.) It changed frequency unpredictably. It sputtered sporadically. It throbbed continuously. But mostly it ground her nerves into mush.

Imagine standing next to a transport truck with its diesel engine idling loudly. Imagine that it's not a very well-tuned engine, so it doesn't make a steady hum or even a steady growl that might eventually disappear from consciousness. Imagine that it has just enough variation to keep your attention.

And imagine that *it never stops.*

Why a generator had to be on twenty-four hours a day, she had no idea.

Why it had to be situated on the lake side was an even greater puzzle.

And why it couldn't be enclosed in any sort of soundproof housing was beyond her.

You'd think the gas would cost more than the outstanding hydro bill, but maybe that's just the way she did math.

That was the summer she bought four more pairs of headphones and four more portable CD players: in addition to the set (earplugs, headphones, and CD player) down at the water, she now had a set in the screened porch, another on the deck, and another in her kayak; the last set was a spare. Just in case. She loaded each CD player with the most masking kind of music she could find. Turned out to be new age stuff mostly. Gentle music with a background of waves lapping, beaver slapping, loons calling...

It was at about this time that she realized the cove and peninsula weren't crown land. Well, not all of it. Walter, one of the three on top of the hill, owned it. It was more or less connected to his house lot. He was, or at least had been for the last fifteen years, content to do nothing with it, which was perfect as far as she was concerned, but since it was so very important to her, she told him she'd love to buy it if he ever wanted to sell it.

He wasn't interested in selling. He said his own lot was worth more with the cove and peninsula attached.

Was he planning to sell? No, he meant when he died.

But you'll be dead, she wanted to say, what do you care how much it'll be worth?

And anyway, how could he know the two lots were worth more together when he didn't know how much she was willing to pay for just the one?

Alas, she let it go, since she really didn't have the money anyway.

Two days later he died.

And his next-door neighbour, one of the other three on the top of the hill, inherited it. At least that's what she thought at first. She later found out that Walter had left it to a friend of his, an elderly gentleman. Who thought it should go to Walter's relatives instead, so he contacted the brother in Austria. Who didn't want it because of the tax implications. Somehow Karl, Walter's neighbour, knew all this and flew to Austria. He came back with the property. For nothing. Or close to.

Anyway, one morning she saw Karl down on the peninsula, right across from her, clearing away some of the lovely foliage that acted as her visual and acoustic screen, keeping what was behind the peninsula out of sight and out of hearing. She paddled over and casually asked, "So what are your plans for this?"

"None of your business!" he screamed at her. "It's *my* property!"

Even so, it *is* my business, she thought. When she'd righted herself, having toppled over from the blast. If it affects me, it's my business. The stakeholder model.

Furthermore, she questioned any argument that derives absolute, or even non-absolute, rights from ownership.

She also questioned ownership based on monetary payment; isn't it wiser to say that whoever appreciates and takes care of something is the owner?

However, she sensed that this was neither the time nor the place to engage him in those discussions.

"Sell it to me then," she said, reasonably enough, "and it'll be *my* property."

"Get away from here!" he screamed, waving the machete he'd been using. "This is *mine*!"

She pretended he hadn't gone momentarily psycho. (There's a backstory: briefly, right after Walter died, she and Karl agreed to share custody of Kodiak, Walter's dog, until she could find a good home for him, and one day, when she and Shiggles went to get Kodiak for their afternoon walk—something they had been doing for years, since Walter was unable to go very far, and Kodiak, being a young German Shepherd, was clearly up for their five miles into forest—Karl had just come out of the bush with him, and Kodiak, having scented her and Shiggles, but not having seen them in the driveway at his house, took off down the hill 'after' them, pointedly not listening to Karl when he called to him; Karl, displaying impressive logic, became angry at her for having witnessed his emasculation. By a dog.)

The lot consisting of the peninsula and the wrap-around end of the cove was assessed at $23,000. She offered Karl $25,000. Then $50,000. Then $75,000. The real estate agent intimated that anything less than $100,000 wouldn't even be considered. The wrap-around end of the cove was near-cliff, the way down to the peninsula from the house was steep and roundabout, and the peninsula itself was too narrow for anything, she thought, so it would probably always stay as is—just a parcel of land attached to the house lot on top of the hill. She didn't have $100,000.

A year later, she was awakened by a chainsaw that sounded like it was right outside her bedroom window. She got up to investigate and was horrified to see that Karl had driven his jeep down the I-guess-it's-not-that-steep-after-all hill and had parked it on the I-guess-there's-more-room-there-than-I-thought peninsula.

He was cutting down the trees.

As quickly as she could, she paddled over, still in her pjs, and begged him to stop. She explained how very important the view was to her, how she spent all day just breathing in its beauty, how it was the raison d'être for—

He said he was clearing it for a boathouse and a dock. She suspected the real estate agent had told him that that would make it more attractive to potential buyers. Apparently there had been not one offer in the year it had been up for sale. She wasn't surprised. They were calling it waterfront. So when people showed up, they understandably looked around in confusion for the water. When they were told that it was five hundred meters down and around and over, they probably got back into their car without even looking at the house.

"But," she said to Karl, "what if the next people don't *want* a boathouse and dock? Or what if they do, but not right *here*?" (Maybe they'll put it further down the peninsula, she hoped, out of her sight.) "Why not let *them* decide what they want to do with this?"

He ignored her. The chainsaw continued to roar.

"They might love the trees as much as I do," she persisted, shouting to be heard. "You might be *decreasing* its value to prospective buyers."

He continued to ignore her.

"*Please*, just *wait a minute*— You have no idea what— Once you cut them down, you can't put them back up! Karl, *I'm begging you*—"

Completely ignored her.

Even though, by this time, she was actually sobbing.

Later that day, she invited Karl and his wife down to her place for tea so he could see what she was talking about when she went on and on about the view—because it really did look different from the inside: from the outside, it looked like there was no view to speak of. She could show him how important it was to her, how she spent all day, every day, whether inside on the couch, or in the screened porch, or on the deck, just looking out at the nothing-but-trees-and-water, it wasn't just a beautiful view, it was integral to the wildernessey solitude ambience that was, in turn, integral to her very life—

He said he didn't have time.

A few days after that, she heard him further along the cove, toward her. With his chainsaw. Was he going to cut down the whole cove?

Surely, she thought, there were laws against that. It was so steep that without the trees' roots, the whole thing would just collapse, crumble, and wash away into the lake. Even if he took down just one or two trees, the rest would follow, a few with every wind.

She called the Township, the Ministry of the Environment, the Ministry of Natural Resources, and Ontario Hydro (they had a line going through it), all the while hearing the chainsaw roar. Finally she got through to a real person by selecting the 'Complaint' option on one of the phone menus. She said right away that she wasn't making a complaint so much as seeking information about what could and could not be done on one's private property, waterfront, and proceeded to explain the situation. The man said he'd come out right away. She was surprised.

On her way into town—she was afraid that if she stayed, she would have gone over and thrown herself around the largest tree, only to experience multiple amputations, followed by decapitation—she saw a Ministry vehicle pull into Walter's driveway. Karl was there, putting away his chainsaw. Lunch break?

On her way back, she pulled into Karl's driveway. She'd had another idea: he wouldn't sell the peninsula and cove part to her, but maybe if she offered to pay the taxes until he sold the whole property, he would at least agree not to cut down any more trees in the interim.

"Hey, Karl, I have an idea," she said as she got out of her car and walked toward him, crouched beside his car. She proceeded to present her offer. He continued to polish his car.

Then he got up slowly and said, "Someone called the Ministry and made a complaint about me cutting down a tree. On *my* property!" He was angry, she realized then. Of course.

She told him that she hadn't made a complaint per se, she had merely asked for information. Because in some places you *can't* cut down trees even on your own property unless…

Actually, he was enraged, she realized belatedly. His accent had made it hard to tell. He started pushing her, and flicking his rag at her. (Good thing he hadn't had his machete in his hand. She later found out that during a previous tantrum, he'd whipped a pipe wrench at someone.)

"Get off my property!!" He kept pushing her, even though she was getting back into her car as quickly as she could.

"FUCKING CUNT!" He slammed her car door against her just-barely-inside foot.

Then as she turned on the ignition, he reached in through the open back window and smacked Shiggles really hard.

It was then that she bought the pepper spray.

Fortunately, snow started to fall early that year, and Karl put his chainsaw away for the winter.

In the spring, he listed the property with another agent, at $295,000. Down from $395,000. She considered making an offer. For the whole thing. She'd sever the two lots, keep the peninsula and cove part, and sell the house part. But by then it wasn't clear that severance would be permitted. The office in charge told her they couldn't make a severance decision until they received an application, and you couldn't apply for a severance until you owned the property. Pure Kafka. So she decided against the purchase. It was a huge financial risk. She'd have to borrow the money, of course, and she'd have to put up her own cabin as collateral. What if she couldn't sever? And what if she couldn't resell for what she'd paid? Loss or not, she'd be back at square one, hoping the next owner would leave the peninsula and cove as is.

So she crossed her fingers and held her breath, hoping that anyone who really intended to make use of the waterfront would buy a lot with a more accessible waterfront, and that anyone who would buy this lot would, like Walter, just enjoy seeing forest and distant water out their window.

TurboJetslams

Then the Taylors bought a lot just behind the peninsula. She didn't even know there was a lot there. She knew, by now, that there was Arnie Willought's cabin and, a bit closer to her, just below Walter's house, a lot with a trailer and a motorcycle on it. She didn't know that the land between the two was a separate lot. It couldn't've been more than 75 feet by 75 feet. But it was waterfront. Technically speaking. It's just that the water was about 100 feet down. Straight down.

Maybe it was because the famed 'Cottage Country' just south of her had become full, or maybe it was because the highway from Toronto had been four-laned, or maybe it was because real estate agents had started calling her neighborhood a "recreational area"—why else would anyone even *consider* buying, and building on, such a lot?

They hired a local guy to do the construction, which was good as far as she was concerned. Because at least she knew the whine of the circular saws and the zztt-zztt of the nail guns and the thrumming of the compressor and the whirr of the drills would stop at five. Which was not the case when someone decided to save money and do it themselves. (More on that later.)

Anticipating that what they were building might further ruin her beautiful, still-stop-and-look-just-*look* view, she went over early on to chat. She explained that she lived—*lived*—she wasn't just a weekender, she was there every day, all day—across the cove from them, just through the trees. She also explained that she treasured so very much the view of nothing but trees, so could they, would they, consider cutting down as few as possible?

"Sure, no problem," the guy, Colin, said. "We love the view too, that's why we bought the place."

Turned out it wasn't a cottage they were building, it was a three-storey house. (For the weekends.) Marble counters in the kitchen, slate tile in the bathroom, and—a bright red metal roof. Once the leaves fell, from October to May, she couldn't help but see it. Every day. All day. Whenever she looked out the window. Any window.

Well, fuck that, she thought. She found a tall thin tree that had fallen, wired a bunch of evergreen branches near the top, then snuggled it to one of her own trees. Took half the day to get the placement just right, but she didn't see the bright red metal roof anymore. At least not when she was on her couch.

She wondered then how someone could afford not just one house but two houses. The second of which was 'nicer' than her only house. Even after fifteen years' work.

And he supported not just himself, she noted, but another adult and two kids.

And he had enough left over for a mini-van, a regular car, a jeep, an ATV, a canoe, a little motor boat, and a pontoon party barge. (More on that later.)

Then the Levines bought one of the cottages previously owned by a quiet, child-free, canoe-loving couple.

The Levines were none of the above.

The Levines had two kids. Both of them screamers. You know the kind. Remember that *Big Bang Theory* episode when Penny and Amy discover the mouse in the chair they'd gotten off the street? That kind of scream.

Sometimes at nine o'clock in the morning.

Sometimes at ten o'clock at night.

And almost always from noon to six.

Furthermore, thanks to Karl and the acoustic corridor he'd cut on the peninsula, she could hear everything the Taylors and the Levines said when they were down at the water. And when they were on their decks up at their houses. And when they were outside at their firepits. In each case, as clearly as if they were standing just outside her screened porch.

Interestingly enough, she seldom heard the women. So it's not like it was impossible to speak and *not* be heard half a mile away. (And it was certainly not impossible not to scream.) But, she thought to herself, men feel so fucking entitled to be heard. They are so convinced of their importance. They could speak quietly if they wanted to; they don't *have* to project. But they do. Whenever they open their mouths. They must dominate. The world.

Certainly, Paradise Lake.

Then the Taylors met the Levines. Rather, the Taylor kids met the Levine kids. The consequence, measured in terms of screaming, illustrated perfectly the concept of the whole being more than the sum of the parts.

Did they let their kids do that back home in the city? Shriek loudly enough for everyone within a square mile to hear them? She doubted it. Their neighbours would be banging on their doors. So why did they let them do it here? Perhaps because those of us who live here are so quiet, they don't even know we're here. Perhaps they think they're the only ones here.

True, their kids' screams probably wouldn't carry a mile back home, she thought, given the obstacles and background noise, but you've got to take the context into consideration. It's like whispering in libraries.

Actually, now that she thought about it, people don't do that anymore either. Last time she was in the local library, doing research for a piece on free speech, the kid at the computer next to her was playing some online game and shouting "Kill the motherfucker!" every ten seconds.

Next time, she drove all the way to the university library and had to listen to a ten-minute cellphone conversation about whether Kevin really meant what he said.

Or maybe they didn't. Think they were the only ones here. Because they both locked their vehicles. With a remote. (What, using a key is too difficult?) She knew this because she heard their car horns confirm the lock on Friday shortly after they arrived. Then she'd hear a horn confirm an unlock later ten minutes later when one of them went back out for something they forgot. Then she'd hear the horn *again*, again confirming the lock. And then half an hour later, when one of the kids wanted something out of the car…

September. Ah. The Taylors and the Levines were gone. Finally. So was everyone else. Fall had become the best time of the year. She had the lake pretty much to herself again.

Some days she'd hear a chainsaw. One or two people bought their firewood in logs and cut it up themselves to save money. It was more painful for her that way.

And some days she'd hear the Township grading the road, the huge tractor thing slowly inching its way down the hill to the end of Campbell's road and back up.

But otherwise, life was good again.

Then one morning when she looked out her cabin, she saw an aluminum boat glaring in the sun. It was right across from her. Smack dab in the center of—right across from her.

Someone had bought Walter's property.

She walked by the house several days in a row, but never saw anyone. It was probably someone from the city, she thought. They had probably come up to close the deal, put their boat down at the water as a sort of claim stake, then returned to the city. Probably wouldn't be up again for weeks.

So the next time she was out paddling, she went across and put a dark green tarp, the one she used to protect her screened porch during the winter, over the aluminum boat, carefully tucking it under the corners.

Back at her cabin, she looked out. Barely noticed it. Smiled. It would save them a lot of bailing as well.

When they came back up, she'd ask if they'd consider moving the boat another ten feet up the peninsula, where it would be out of her view altogether, but this was a great interim solution.

In fact, she had another great solution. A great permanent solution. The lot just below Walter's house, the one with the trailer and motorcycle, was for sale. The new people could buy that property and sell the peninsula and cove to her. She'd pay whatever they had to pay. So it wouldn't cost them anything. She'd offer to pay all the incidental fees as well. They'd still have waterfront. And it would be right in front of them, not down and around out of sight. It was steep, but there was already a staircase down to the shore. True, the water was a bit muckier there, being between the main shore and the peninsula, but if they were just planning to go boating, not swimming, that wouldn't be a problem. It was a win-win-win: she'd get what she wanted; the new people would still have what they wanted; and the trailer and motorcycle guy would get what he wanted.

So as soon as she saw someone at the house, she stopped by. She introduced herself to the woman who was unloading some stuff, explained that she was the one who had covered their boat, and explained why, then made her offer about the property switch. Janet said she'd consider it.

Jim, her husband, said no. He scoffed, saying you'd have to be a mountain goat to get down to the water from the other lot. (Vic realized later that what he meant was you'd have to be minimally fit to handle the stairs. Apparently he needed to be able to drive down to the water on his ATV. Which he could do via the cove-peninsula lot, thanks to Karl.)

But she came to understand that the real reason he rejected her proposal was that he was pissed off at her for having had the nerve to go onto *his* property and cover *his* boat. Apparently that had really *really* pissed him off.

She never understood it. The closest she came was to assume a variant of 'My car, my penis.'

In fact, he was so pissed off, he removed the tarp. And left the boat there. Not only all summer, but also all winter. All winter, the aluminum boat sat in the snow and reflected the sun like crazy.

She slowly came to realize that she'd be seeing it every time she looked out at the trees and the water. No matter where she was, inside or outside. *For the rest of her life.*

She became deeply depressed.

And so fucking angry! He had over ten acres. There was no frickin' reason he couldn't store his boat somewhere else over the winter. Even in the summer, there was no reason he couldn't throw a tarp over it. He used it maybe once a month, to take his kids out for a ride when their friends were over.

She tried once more, explaining how the sun reflected off it, how it was right in the middle of—

"I have a right to do whatever I want on my own property," he insisted. "No one else is complaining."

Rights are not absolute, she wanted to say.

Rights are attached to responsibilities, she wanted to say. You can't have one without the other. You shouldn't be able to.

It's not a matter of rights, she wanted to say, but a matter of courtesy.

Suppose Karl parked his old RV, she wanted to say, exactly where it blocked the satellite signal just enough to make a can't-help-but-see-it blank spot in the middle of your tv screen. Suppose that moving your tv would make no difference, and you couldn't switch satellite tv providers because there is only the one. And suppose, further, that Karl had a huge parking area in front of his three-car garage. Would you not, should you not, go him and say, 'Hey, Karl, your RV is blocking the satellite signal, and I really really enjoy watching the game every night, and the kids watch their programs, we have a tv room, we spend a lot of time there, couldn't you please park your RV just ten feet to the left?' Would you really shrug and say he has the right to do whatever he wants on his own property? And just accept that you'd have to watch tv with a blank spot in the middle of the screen *for the rest of your life?*

But it was clear he wasn't interested in anything she wanted to say.

And that wasn't all.

Although the house had seemed in pretty good shape to her, Janet and Jim apparently thought otherwise. So for the next two months, five days a week, eight hours a day, she heard circular saws, nail guns, power drills, compressors, a machine from hell that blew insulation, and my god, instead of just buying new flooring, they bought rough planks and had them planed them on site, with a portable planing mill.

There are zoning laws separating residential from industrial for a reason, she thought.

Finally all the outdoor work done. (As far as she could tell, just a wrap-around deck. Which, unfortunately, wrapped around to her side.) But she was *still* hearing— She went up to investigate. The guys were indeed working inside at that point, but the door facing her was wide open. She explained that she was one shredded nerve away from being jello, could they at least close the door when they were working inside?

Well, no, apparently they could not. They told Jim about her visit, her request, and he was indignant. How dare she ask the workers *he'd* hired to do something like that? How dare she *talk* to the workers *he'd* hired!

She wondered if it was a 'My workers, my penis' sort of thing.

And *that* wasn't all.

He'd decided to install a ground heat system. While she applauded, simultaneously doubting, his concern for the environment, it required four trenches to be dug. Which required, first, that the chunk of forest beside the house come down. Walter would have been appalled. But so what. He was dead. She was not. The trees were downed and the trenches were dug. With a *backhoe.*

Jim had his own backhoe.

What are the odds, she asked herself, curled into a tight coil under her desk like a disturbed centipede, keening, rocking back and forth, that not one but two residents on such a small acoustically-challenged lake would own their own backhoes?

As soon as the hired guys left at five, Jim came home and started on the trenches. He'd go until around ten. Eight in the morning until ten at night. Noise. Gawdawful machinery engine banging clanging scraping noise.

But not every day.

So she asked him, shouting (he'd left the backhoe idling) (a mere ten feet away), "Could you let me know which days you'll be digging your trenches? I kayak up the river to escape the eight-to-five noise, and if I know which days you're going to be at it, I'll just stay there, up the river, until dark."

Well, he couldn't say.

"Why not?" she hollered.

He didn't know.

"You don't know what days you're going to work on the trenches? Not even at, say, noon that day?" she screamed.

No.

Apparently he doesn't know that he's going to do something until he does it.

She was stunned. And again, speechless. What do you say to that?

He'd gone to the Township, he said; there were no noise by-laws.

Part of her wanted to explain the inadequacy of legal moralism: just because something's legal doesn't mean it's right.

The other part of her wanted to explain that if he had to ask about noise bylaws, HE WAS MAKING TOO MUCH FUCKING NOISE!

"It is what it is," he summarized, dismissing her.

What? What the hell does that mean? It is what it is.

By November, he'd been at it for over two months, but he'd gotten just three trenches done. He was running out of time. It would snow soon. So he hired the local outfit to do the fourth trench. They arrived in the morning with one of those new mini-excavator things. It had an enclosed engine. (They can do that? Enclose the engine?) It had a muffler. (They can do that? Put a muffler on an excavator?) So she hardly heard it.

And the remaining trench took the little machine a day. *A day.*

Early the following summer, on the May long weekend, when she heard the TurboJetslams circling in the next around-the-corner cove, despite Lyle's backhoe and screaming kids reverberating in her own cove, it suddenly occurred to her. What if the Taylors got jetslams? What if the Levines got jetslams?

What if the Taylors *and* the Levines got jetslams?

And what if the long stretches of forest on either side of the lake from halfway down to the end weren't stretches of crown land, but private properties already subdivided into teeny tiny lots? Now easily accessible thanks to the road Tim and Lyle had made?

She saw the writing on the wall.

It said "YOU ARE SO FUCKED."

So she prepared a carefully written petition to present to the Township:

Given the small size of Paradise Lake, combined with its acoustics due to the surrounding hills, and given the damage caused by fossil fuel emissions both into the air and into the water (two-stroke engines release up to 30% of their fuel uncombusted, which is 118 times that released by cars), I propose the following in order to preserve the natural environment and at the same allow the current residents to enjoy said natural environment.

1. No motorized vehicles on the lake. There are two large lakes with-

in a ten-minute drive on which jetslammers can race around to their heart's content and never be near enough to shore to annoy anyone. Or kill them. Snowmobilers can use the trails set aside just for them, accessible five minutes away on Fisher Road.

2. No dirt bikes, ATVs, or snowmobiles on roads or trails other than the designated snowmobile trails (which, I assume, double as ATV and dirt bike trails). Since there are no sidewalks, people walk on the roads and would like to do so safely. Without earplugs. Or noseplugs. The same goes for use of the trails, not only by people walking, but also by people on snowshoes and cross-country skis.

3. No further construction on Paradise Lake. Failing that, construction noise to be limited to Monday to Friday, nine to five. This includes, but is not limited to, the use of nail guns, power drills, impact drivers, angle grinders, pneumatic torque wrenches, belt sanders, disc sanders, circular saws, bandsaws, air compressors, and portable planing mills. And backhoes.

4. Regular maintenance noise to be limited to Saturday afternoons. This includes, but is not limited to, the use of lawnmowers, weed trimmers, leaf blowers, chainsaws, and woodchippers.

5. Gas-powered generators to be used only when the power is out for more than twenty-four hours. If people can't do without their tvs for twenty-four hours, they should get a solar back-up system. And learn to read.

Anyone who violates these bylaws should have their offending machine confiscated. And their cottage. And then they should die a horrible, horrible death inspired by the masters of the middle ages. From which they have clearly come.

She received a response from the Township informing her that it was their policy not to act on petitions unless they were signed by a minimum of ten people. Apparently the default mode was 'Do whatever the fuck you want' and special application had to be made to *prevent* forementioned whatever the fuck. Rather than the other way around.

Ten people? There were only twelve permanent residents on the lake. Double the number when she first moved in, but still. And three seasonals for every permanent made forty-eight households altogether.

All right then, could she have the Township's mailing list so she could get on that?

No. Due to the Access of Information Act, they were not allowed to give out that information.

Okay, names and phone numbers then?

No. Due to the Access of Information Act, they were not allowed to give out that information.

So she had to go door to door?

Like she was going to do that.

In any case, she'd managed to piss off all but three of the permanent residents. Well, she thought, maybe she could get those three on board, and they could get another six.

The first people she visited hadn't noticed any noise.

What? How can you not hear a backhoe scraping on the rock? How can you not hear screaming kids, chainsaws— She had to shout to be heard above their tv. It was a 48" flat-screen mounted above the fireplace.

Nor had they noticed the sudden appearance of a bright red roof among the trees, they said, staring at the tv, their backs to the lakeside windows.

And anyway, they added, you can't go around telling people what they can and cannot do on their own property.

Inside the second house, it was the same. Despite windows on the lake side, all of the furniture was turned to face the 72" flat-screened tv. Who needs Big Brother?

Big Brother? We don't watch that.

What? Doesn't *anyone* read anymore?

Come to think of it, she'd never seen anyone else sit down at the water with a book in hand. In fact, she'd never seen anyone else sit down at the water, period. Why did they all live here then?

No one was home at the third house either.

Which was probably why they actually *liked* noise.

So, she realized, those of us who see things, who hear things, those of us who pay attention to what's around us, we're the ones to suffer. The desensitized dullards, the mentally lazy, the ones who go through life oblivious, they're not feeling any pain.

But what happens then is the more noise there is, the more people will tune out and *not* pay attention (at least those who can do that, she thought with some envy); and the more people *aren't* paying attention, the louder you have to be to *get* their attention; and the louder you are, the more people will tune out...

She could see she was on her own. It would be up to her to right the wrongs of the universe. Well, she thought philosophically, who better than an ethics professor?

And, as she had been told repeatedly by her ex, no one had a keener sense of injustice.

So, about that pontoon party barge... Since the Taylors' new summer house didn't quite clear the peninsula, the water right in front of them was on the stagnant side. Not anything you'd want to swim in. Why they bought the lot they did, given their two kids and summer fun plans, she had no idea.

Their first solution was to drive to Weshin Lake, which had a public beach. Sort of. It was pretty pathetic. Certainly didn't go with the marble counters in their kitchen.

Their second solution was to buy a pontoon boat and use it as a party barge. Problem was they'd park it in front of someone's house—someone *else's* house—and then proceed to act like no one lived there. Invariably, they'd do this when they'd invited another couple, with kids, to their 'cottage'. So all the kids would use the boat as a swimming raft, shrieking and hollering as they jumped into the water, then climbed back up, then jumped in again, while the parents would sit, drinks in hand, talking. In front of *her* house. *Her* home.

Never when she was actually right there on her dockraft, but when she was up on her deck or in her screened porch.

One bright day, after five minutes of this, she got her little bullhorn—ya gotta love eBay—and called out to them.

"I don't know where you left your hat.

"I don't care how cold the water is.

"It doesn't matter to me whether or not you buy marshmallows when you go into town.

"And I don't give a rat's ass what you plan to say to Mark when you get back to the office."

There was a moment of silence.

And then the motor started up.

That was easy, she thought.

Too easy, she realized. The following weekend. When they parked again in front of her house. Since they had no guests to impress with maturity.

Often, she just went for a long walk in the forest. (It was either that or go inside and close all the windows.) As mentioned, there was an old logging road at the top of the hill that led into the forest. About half a mile in, the road went past a one-room cabin, but early on she'd obtained permission from the guy who owned it to walk past, presumably trespassing, in order to continue on to the massive chunk of crown land; in theory, she could walk all the way to Algonquin Park.

Shiggles loved it, she loved it, it was quiet, and it was beautiful.

One day on her way back home, she saw, couldn't help but see, a bright red and white sign for the local franchise of a large hardware store chain, nailed onto the tree at the fork in the road (the Campbells' new road on the right going to their house, the lane on the left going to her house, the Johnsons', and the Dreshers').

What the hell? She bristled the rest of the way home.

Advertising in public places should be illegal, she thought. It's an invasive assault on people's consciousness. And for those who aren't conscious, it's an insidious manipulation of their subconscious. Of course people will deny that, but that just proved her point.

It should especially be illegal in places of beauty. It was a sad, sad day when arenas started allowing advertisements all along the rink sides and even on the ice. Years to achieve the perfect line for a spiral destroyed by a bright graphic in the background clamoring about fruit juice.

Her second fireplace insert had had the company name etched on the glass. Since she liked to watch a fire without having someone's name etched on her consciousness, she'd had the glass replaced.

She was tired, she told herself, of breath-taking vistas of forest, water, sun, and sky being destroyed by someone's crass and selfish desire for money. Why do we never say 'No' to business here in Canada and the States? Because we have no values other than the pursuit of profit? Because we consider that to be the supreme value, the one that trumps all other values? Seriously? Do we really?

Or is it that most people here have no sense of beauty? Like the guy who keeps tossing aside my rocks at the spring, are most Canadians and Americans simply aesthetically challenged? If you can't see it, you can't see when it's ruined. But if you can't see the natural beauty of the place, you shouldn't live here. People who don't appreciate Beethoven shouldn't go to concerts and talk all the way through.

Imagine a 'No Advertising' rule: whenever you wanted to buy something, you'd just look it up in a central directory with a really good search engine that enabled you to see all of your options (a select few based on your preferences) accompanied by product information and customer reviews. Freed from the constant onslaught of others telling us what we need and want, maybe we could recognize our genuine needs and wants.

When she got home, she wrote a letter to the hardware store:

> *What right do you have to shout "BUY MY STUFF, MAKE ME RICH!" in my face two or three times a day? Do you seriously think you have a right to pursue profit by any means? If so, on what grounds? And, if so, do you believe that that right is absolute—that it trumps all other rights and/or the rights of all other people? In short, how do you justify your behavior?*
>
> *If the moral questions presented above don't persuade you that your action is indefensible, let me approach the issue from the perspective of sheer marketing: what's the point of the bright red sign you've nailed to the tree at the intersection of Paradise Lake Lane and Campbell's Road? There are four people who live here (both roads are dead ends), and we all know you exist. Either we already buy your stuff (or did until you shoved your sign in our face) or we don't (and certainly won't start now). So why the hell have you done it?*
>
> *It's a residential area, for god's sake. It's bad enough that we have to see your signs on the highway. (Where they distract us, intentionally, from driving. Thank you very much. Hope your kid gets killed by a driver who had half his attention grabbed by a neon sign blinking at him to buy someone else's stuff.) But now we have to see it on our*

laneway?

You also shout "BUY MY STUFF, MAKE ME RICH" at us by mail. In a multi-page format, no less. (You obviously think you have the right to waste a lot of natural resources and a lot of people's time and energy. Who the hell do you think you are?)

Are you going to start calling me on the phone too? That's harassment.

And so is the sign you now force me to see several times a day.

Next time she walked by the one-room cabin, the guy's son was there. Frank. Or, as she liked to call him now, Frankie. He stood on the road, belligerence personified, arms crossed, facing her.

"You can't go through here anymore."

"Oh." Had there been too many dirt bikes and ATVs? She knew that he hated the snowmobiles whizzing past his place in the winter; there were remnants of a gate across the road. "You're putting up the gate again?"

"No. Just you. *You* can't come through here anymore."

She was puzzled. Surely she was the *least* intrusive. She didn't make any noise, and she certainly didn't toss any beer cans onto his property.

"You don't like what I do, so I don't like what you do."

Ah. He was part owner, by marriage, of the hardware store. She'd forgotten that.

According to Kohlberg, the reciprocation model of morality Frank had chosen to embrace was typical of two-year-olds. She was about to say that when the rest of her brain came online. He was cutting her off from the beautiful, quiet forest. She couldn't go for long walks anymore. She couldn't escape the noise at the lake.

"I'm sorry," she said. Truly she was. If she'd known the price of writing the letter, she would've just taken down the sign in the middle of the night.

She tried to reconcile, to remedy the situation, to explain that the advertisement was intrusive and just plain stupid. He didn't care. After two minutes, he turned away.

"I can't stand here and talk all day, I've got work to do," he said.

Oh well then. The man has work to do. And god knows, the work men do is always more important than anything, anyone, else.

She hated when that happened.

So the next time, she made her way into the forest from the bottom of the hill. It took three times as long. And it wasn't pleasant. She ended up scratched all to hell and missing an eye.

Then while she was heading up one of the side trails to the first of the two small lakes, a pair of ATVs coming from the lake stopped and blocked her path.

"What part of 'No Trespassing' don't you understand?" the first man shouted at her angrily.

"What?" Hello to you too.

"Frank told you you couldn't walk on his property anymore."

"Yeah…" She saw that they had hunting rifles sticking out of the backs of their vehicles. It was open season on something or other. She picked up Shiggles and held her close.

"This is his property, so what part of 'No Trespassing' don't you understand?"

"Oh. I thought this was crown land."

"Don't give me that. You *know* this is his property."

"No, I don't. How would I?" How does he know what I know and don't know? How does he know who I am?

This was not going well.

"You *know* this is his property," the guy insisted. The guy behind him started to look uncomfortable. "So what part of 'No Trespassing' don't you understand?"

"I told you, I thought this was crown land."

"No, I want to know what part of 'No Trespassing' don't you understand?!"

Not going well at all.

"I don't have time for this," she said then, turning away. "I've got work to do."

One of the guns went off.

Okay, shouldn't have said that last bit.

So she went into the Township office to take a good look at the map they had on the wall. The side trail she'd been on was indeed on Frank's property. Okay then.

She carefully examined the map. If she entered at the bottom of the hill and stayed to the left, she'd be on crown land all the way in and out. Good.

No, wait a minute. She looked again at the map. What the hell?

"What's this thick black line here?" she asked the clerk.

"That's the public access road."

"And it goes right *through* this guy's private property?"

The little shit.

"Thanks," she said and headed for the door.

"Oh," she stopped. "Are there any bylaws in this Township about signage?"

Of course not. Bylaws? In this township?

She went home, logged on to one of those online sign shops that real estate companies use, and ordered a sign for—well, she thought long and hard about it. The customer service person had some concern, but she told him that it would be posted in Canada and they had different copyright laws there. Which was true, strictly speaking.

Next day, while Frank was at work, at his hardware store, she erected a sign right across from his house, advertising a cure for erectile dysfunction.

He took it down that very same day.

All right then.

She took down the hardware sign the very next day.

Even so, she started walking on the road on the weekends. Tim and Lyle had taken to racing through the crown land on their dirt bikes every weekend. Probably needed a break from all that backhoe work.

Although she could hear them from a mile away—well, from five miles away actually, since they had two-strokes without mufflers—and so could get off the trail and out of their way, it meant she had to walk the rest of the way in their fume trail, whether she kept going or turned around. Either way, she'd have a headache by the time she got back home.

She knew people thought she was exaggerating when she complained about that, because *they* didn't get headaches from the fumes, despite the fumes' proven neurotoxicity. But that was just because they were missing that part of their brain.

Twice a year she'd take a large garbage bag with her to pick up the litter—mostly beer cans and fast food containers, but often whole plastic bags of garbage had been tossed in among the trees. Quite simply, she didn't want to see it when she went for a walk.

She typically did her litter pick-up after the spring hunt, because hunters threw a lot of shit out of their trucks and off of their ATVs, and again after the summer because it was the summer people, not those who lived there, who tossed candy wrappers and coffee cups onto the roadside.

So one fine day, she and Shiggles headed out, two large garbage bags in hand.

She had always suspected that men littered more than women, and had recently come across a statistic supporting her hunch: males do 72% of deliberate littering and are responsible for 96% of accidental littering.

She wondered why that was so, tossing a Tim Hortons cup into her bag, and hypothesized that it was because 'cleaning up after' is seen as a woman's task. After all, wasn't it Mom who cleaned up after them when they were kids? (Mom did the cleaning; Dad did the fixing.) Of course the generalization from Mom to all women was a mistake: 'Mom cleaned up after me, Mom is a woman, so women should clean up after me' is the same as 'Princess is a kitten, Princess is white, so white things should be kittens'. But she doubted these morons could think in a—well, she doubted these morons could think.

Of course a mistake was also made in thinking that when you're old enough to drink beer and buy your own fast food, you're still a kid who needs Mom or a woman to clean up after you. No, wait, she was making the mistake there—she was confusing chronological age with developmental age.

She put her thoughts on pause when she heard a pick-up truck approach. Ever since Bullert had come at her, she was super vigilant. (More on that later.) The pick-up was green though (Bullert's was black), and it was going slow. Quite slow, in fact. When it got to her and Shiggles, the driver called out, "'Atta girl, glad to see you're good for something!"

What?

She stared at the disappearing truck. He seemed to know her. But she hadn't recognized him. Maybe he was one of the guys in the fishing boats that piss her off so much. They all looked the same to her.

'Glad to see you're good for something'?

She refused to pick up one more piece of garbage. Left the half-filled bags where they were and turned home.

A few days later, on her way to the library, she saw it. The green pick-up. It was parked at a white house a couple miles toward town. The mailbox said Cobbs. Didn't ring a bell. Didn't matter. The guy had a problem. She had a solution.

Two weeks later—she figured he would've made similar cracks to his current girlfriend, his current wife, and all of his exes by then—she headed out after midnight, parked a hundred feet from his place, and carried from there her two half-filled bags of garbage. (They'd remained where she'd left them. Stewing in the sun.) She upended both of them into the front seat of his pick-up, then tossed onto the dash the rabbit Shiggles had killed the night before. Given what had happened the time she'd put one of Shiggles' kills on top of her car—if she'd've buried it, Shiggles would've just dug it up again, so she'd intended, but then forgotten, to take it to the dump that afternoon—his pick-up would be crawling with maggots by morning.

Shortly after, she happened to notice the fridge sitting in her shed. It was the huge one that had come with the cabin when she bought it. Oddly enough, it was one of those stainless steel ones.

So she called George, the guy-for-hire in town who did all sorts of odd jobs, and asked him to take the fridge. Not to the dump, but to the property below the Millers. She told George that she knew the guy, and that he wanted to buy the fridge from her, second-hand.

She'd carefully examined the surveyor's map she had from when she'd bought her cabin, and saw that the trailer-and-motorcycle lot was almost as weirdly shaped as the Millers' lot. Although they couldn't see the trailer and motorcycle from their new, enlarged kitchen window and the adjoining screened-in part of the wrap-around deck—presumably intended for barbecues and sunsets and what have you—and although most of their view was of the slope going down to the water, there was actually one section of the level part of the other guy's lot that extended into their view.

That's where she had George put the fridge.

On a Monday morning, when the Millers were at work.

After George left, she consulted the sun, then pushed the fridge over on its side, angled just so.

And left her other dark green tarp crumpled up in a pile right beside it.

Bright and early next morning—just four hours after she'd gone to bed—because she was now working from ten to four, since it was the only time it was quiet, what with the backhoe, the dirt bikes, and the screaming kids—she was awakened by said screaming kids. The Levines and the Taylors must both be up. Again, thanks to Karl and his chainsaw, they sounded like they were right outside her window.

It's like they think this is their own personal amusement park, she grumbled. Maybe their new water slide makes them think so.

Well, a person's gotta do what a person's gotta do. She hauled herself out of bed, grabbed her bullhorn—best eBay purchase she ever made—opened the sliding door a crack, and called out, "WILL YOU PLEASE SHUT THE FUCK UP!"

There was a moment of surprised silence. At least she thought it was surprise.

Then, "Language!" the mother called back. Sweetly.

What? What?!

Part of her wanted to reply, "Yes! You're using language! Words! Signifiers of meaning! You're intruding on my consciousness with meaningful utterances! That my brain involuntarily processes. So if you insist on speaking loudly enough for me to hear, at least do it in Swahili!"

Instead, she shouted into her bullhorn, "I CAN USE WHATEVER LANGUAGE I WANT WHEN I'M ON MY OWN PROPERTY!"

"Yes, but we can hear you!" the mother replied.

There was another moment, a rather long moment, of surprised silence. Followed by Vic's "DUH!"

It's all that DEET, she thought. And two-stroke fumes.

Next day, on her way to get the mail, just as she approached Karl's place, she saw that he was outside, in his driveway. He bent down and called to Shiggles, all nice like he used to do when he was sane.

"DON'T YOU TOUCH HER!" she screamed at him, exploding into a sprint that would impress Florence Griffith-Joyner.

She tackled him, smashed his head into the ground a few times, got up, kicked him hard in the groin, then stomped on each of his knees. It was easy. After all, the guy was seventy.

She increased the time she spent kayaking on the lake, mostly because she could kayak up the river away from the dirt bikes, the backhoe, the screaming kids, and for the two weeks the people in the next cove were up, the jetslams.

There were still many stretches of nothing but forest (though also, increasingly, styrofoam bait cups, cigarette packaging, and beer cans) (all of which she'd pick up and put into the small garbage bag she now kept in her kayak), and she thoroughly enjoyed—no that's not quite the right word—she blissed out on the beauty of it all: the sun sparkling on the water, the breeze rippling through the trees... It made her neurons hum with peace and joy and serotonin.

It was especially amazing in the evening, when the water became glass and everything was just so—still.

Then a little fishing boat motor would start up. She would be able to hear it, a mile away, no matter where she was on the lake. It would be a very loud motor. Probably a very old motor. Definitely a two-stroke motor. The boat would start out, at a snail's pace. She'd sigh, reach for her drybag, and pull out her earplugs, headphones, and iPod (she'd replaced the CD player in her kayak with an iPod). The boat would take half an hour to get half way around the lake. By then, she would have paddled half way up the river and be in blessed silence again.

Until another fishing boat would appear, coming toward her. They'd pass each other, and then she'd have to paddle in his trail of exhaust fumes for a good fifteen minutes. Long enough to get a headache that would last the rest of the day.

So often, an hour later, she'd be back at her dock. She'd get a cup of tea, some ibuprofen, and a good book. Then settle on her dockraft to watch the late afternoon sun set the trees alight.

This was the case when yet another fishing boat motor started up. The boat came toward her place from across the lake. And parked just twenty feet away.

Two guys were in it, fishing. Or getting away from their wives and the kids they'd made.

One guy lit a cigarette. She could tell even though she had her eyes closed in exhausted rage and frustration. Because, of course, she could smell it.

They started talking. It was the most inane conversation in the world.

She joined in. "Why do you enjoy inflicting gratuitous torture on living creatures?"

Okay, it's a bit off-topic, she acknowledged that, but then, really, it was hard to tell. And actually, given what they were doing, it was spot-on.

But they both looked at her as if they were just now seeing her. Sitting there a mere twenty feet away.

Probably they were. Just now seeing her. It never ceased to amaze her how invisible middle-aged women are. To men.

Guess why.

"You trick a fish into biting at a hidden hook," she continued, "by which you then pull it up into the air. Have you ever had a fish hook through your lip? And then had your whole body pulled up by it?"

"It doesn't feel it," the one guy said.

"Sure it does," she said. "When a fish gets stung by a bee, it rubs its mouth on something. Obviously it's feeling it. They grunt when they're given an electric shock. They have a nervous system, and neurons fire in their brain same as ours when they're subjected to painful stimuli.

"On top of that, they start suffocating once you pull them out of the water. What do you think all that thrashing is about? Think they're doing the Macarena?

"And then you handle the thing so much trying to get the hook out—you use barbed hooks, I'll bet—that you end up with half of its slime on you. Slime it needs to protect itself from infection.

"Then you *throw* it back, instead of gently submerging it, and cradling it, until it swims away.

"So it'll probably die. Up to sixty percent do.

"And *then*, in an obvious display of psychopathology, which is normal for males, you call it *sport*."

They thought about all of that. Or not.

"Why don't you mind your own business?" the other guy finally said, annoyed. But not quite sure why.

"I'd love to," she replied. "But you keep shoving *your* business in my face! In my ears! In my head!"

They stared at her.

"So your business becomes my business whether I want it to or not!"

Okay, that probably confused them.

"And I don't!"

They were silent.

"Don't what?" the first guy said.

She sighed.

She'd tried. You see that, right?

"Here, catch!" She threw the dirty ball she'd been fiddling with.

The guy's right hand reached out and caught it.

"Not bad," she said, then quickly closed the book she'd wrapped the fishing line around, and gave it a yank.

"OW! Fuck!"

The hook had also been among that afternoon's lake litter pick-up. She yanked again.

"FUCK!" He practically lurched out of the boat.

He tried to grab the line, succeeded, and got the worst paper cut ever. "OW—SHIT!"

She kept yanking, as his buddy scrambled for the knife to cut the line.

"GODDAMMIT! WHAT THE FUCK ARE YOU DOING?" he yelled at her.

She thought it was pretty clear what she was doing, so she didn't answer.

"HURRY THE FUCK UP!" he hollered at his buddy, who finally managed to cut the line.

"FUCKING BITCH!" he screamed at her then as his buddy started up the motor. "YOU'RE FUCKING CRAZY, YOU KNOW THAT?!" he added, as they roared away from her. Far, far away from her. She smiled.

Next day, another fishing boat parked just a few feet away from her dock. When she was sitting right there. Reading. Did they not recognize the activity?

Three guys—different guys, she was happy to note—or not, since it indicated a seemingly endless supply—were in the boat. As soon as the guy in the back turned off the motor and threw in the anchor, the guy in the front got up from the bench seat and sat on the prow. Perhaps, pressed to explain why, he said to his buddies that he could get a better cast from there. She didn't know for sure, because she had her earplugs in. His lips moved though, so he must've been saying something. Or maybe he was reading the beer can he had in his hand. One more slug finished the can, which he tossed overboard, of course, and a few minutes later he cast and then started to reel in, slowly. He cast again, and reeled in, slowly. He cast again, and reeled in, slowly. *Such* a sport, fishing.

A few minutes later, the second guy 'decided' he'd stand up. If asked, he'd say he was more comfortable standing. He'd be unable to say why exactly, since, physically speaking, it would be so obviously untrue.

As she watched The Idiot Show, as she saw the guy's long, rigid rod sticking out at groin level, as she saw the guy's hand fumbling around the reel tucked in at his crotch, she suddenly realized there was yet another reason men liked to go fishing. It was the same reason they all wanted to play guitar.

A mild discomfort must have spread to the other two, but neither one of them would have been able to explain it. Certainly it wasn't that they were afraid their buddy might fall out of the boat.

Because shortly after, clearly unable to tolerate the subordination one more minute, the other two also stood up. The one sitting on the prow stood up *on the prow.*

They all went overboard. Apparently that was not a foreseeable result.

Could any of them swim?

No.

Were any of them wearing life jackets?

Of course not.

She watched them flail about for a while, then decided to initiate a rescue.

Just as soon as pretty little canaries flew out their asses.

TurboJetslams

A few days later, she tried again. To have a beautiful paddle out on the lake and up the river. She got as far as the marshy section past the second little cove before she heard the shots. BOOM. A minute passed. BOOM. Another minute passed. BOOM. A minute and a half passed. BOOM. Someone was at the shooting range.

Since hearing gun shots while one paddles was not conducive to peace and tranquility, she got out her earplugs, headphones, iPod...

A short while later, she saw a loon rise out of the water, wings spread, mouth open. It must have been sending its distress call.

A minute later, on her headphones—she'd chosen one of Dan Gibson's albums—she heard a loon's beautiful 'I'm here' call.

Not for long, she feared. Clearly distressed.

The following spring, the Johnsons, the elderly couple down the lane, sold their place and moved somewhere closer to, well, everything. Hospitals, mostly, Vic thought.

And they sold their place to some guy named Bullert. Who arrived in a pick-up truck with a trailer holding two ATVs. His friends also arrived in pick-up trucks with ATV-full trailers.

For half an hour, she—no—everyone on the lake heard deafening VROOM-VROOMING as the men made sure their engines were working to their satisfaction.

Or maybe they were just sitting on their ATVs revving their engines for the hell of it.

In any case, she thought, apparently they hadn't gotten the memo about fossil fuel consumption, fossil fuel emissions, and climate change. Impossible as that was, she was sure that half the time they forgot they'd left their ATVs idling. (The times when the VROOM-VROOMING would stop after an hour, but the engines would keep going. For another hour.)

Finally, they took off.

They zoomed down the lane and up the hill. Good riddance.

Then they zoomed back down the hill and up the lane. Forget something? All six of them?

They zoomed back down the lane and up the hill. Good riddance again.

Twenty minutes later—apparently going up and down the hill amused them greatly—she heard them go in the old logging road toward Frankie's place.

They never made it to the snowmobile trail, a wide, groomed trail that cut through the forest from the access road over to Fisher Lake Road, where it then joined with a huge network of trails far from any residential area. Because everyone on Paradise Lake heard them for the next two hours, shifting gears continuously and accelerating in what was the most gas-inefficient way. She knew. Because she used to drive a motorcycle. And she *never* drove it like that.

Before dirt bikes and ATVs were invented, people who wanted to enjoy the natural beauty of the wilderness went for a hike. Now they were too fat to do that. Beer has that effect. Actually, she doubted that ATVing was about enjoying the natural beauty of the wilderness; if it were, ATVers wouldn't throw garbage all over the place, and they wouldn't go so frickin' fast they couldn't even see said natural beauty.

That Sunday evening, when they had all gone home, every curve in the road had speed grooves and gullies. And there were half a dozen places where Bullert and his buddies had apparently driven in circles. The Campbells and the Dreshers were going to have to go very slowly on their way into work. (The grader would go by eventually, smoothing everything out. It did so every week. On Fridays. Just before the weekend.)

She decided to find out how long it would take Bullert to discover a missing spark plug. (What kind of stupid is it to piss off so many people who live 24/7 where you have to leave your house, and all of your stuff, unattended during the week?)

If you needed to replace a missing spark plug, they had them at the hardware store in town, of course, but they happened to be sold out. Fred's garage was also sold out.

Someone had bought them all the day before.

And it was an hour's drive to the city.

She had a lovely long walk in the forest that weekend.

The weekend after that, his ATV ran out of gas about five miles in. (He swore he'd filled the tank the previous Sunday, just before he left.) Apparently it took him forever to walk out. No surprise. Because it's *not* all muscle.

A few days later, a critical part on Tim and Lyle's backhoe went missing. It was a discontinued part and not available anywhere. Not even on eBay.

TurboJetslams

On the Monday, when she and Shiggles went for a walk up the lane—Shiggles liked to say hi to Nutter, Caramel, and Beast, but they didn't go there on weekends because of Bullert—they saw a new dog at the edge of the road. Right across from Bullert's. A big black one.

Correction. They saw a bear at the edge of the road.

Correction. Three bears.

Ah, she thought. A Teddy Bear Picnic.

Next morning, she saw that Bullert and his buddies had tossed a couple garbage bags full of garbage into the bush, into the treed swath of land between the lane and Campbell's road. The swath was actually Andy's property, but she didn't think Bullert realized that. It wasn't *his* property, that's probably all that mattered. Oh well, she thought, looking at the torn plastic, the scattered tins, licked clean, the packaging of various materials, torn and scattered, but also licked clean—let Andy deal with it. Problem is, he probably wouldn't notice it. Since Bullert had dumped it across from his own driveway, not across from Andy's driveway.

Which, by the way, how stupid is that, she asked Shiggles, safe in her arms just in case. Even *you* don't shit in your own yard if you can help it.

He probably also left his barbecue grill outside. Yummy bits of meat and fat. What self-respecting wolf within a hundred miles would ignore that?

It happened every time a new seasonal moved in. They'd just toss their leftover food: hamburger buns, pasta, wieners, vegetable soup, rice, bologna sandwiches, chicken bones— She'd seen it all.

Including a car battery. And a bag full of used diapers. But that was along the road, not beside someone's cottage.

Thing is, would they do that in the city? She didn't think so.

Then why do it here? Do they really not even *consider* the possibility that their actions might have consequences for others? Who might not see Mama Bear, or raccoons, in time to grab their Shiggles?

Maybe they figure it's organic, it'll decompose. (How slow *are* city raccoons?)

Maybe, like so many other things, being here, at a lake, in a forest, brings out the primeval in people. They think they're in the wild. Where there are no dumps.

But where there *are* bears. And wolves. And raccoons. And martens— Anyone in the wild with an ounce of grey matter, let alone moral responsibility, buries their garbage. Or carries it out.

She put on the pair of gloves she'd brought with her and moved all the leftover garbage back onto Bullert's property. Maybe he'd get the message.

The following weekend, late Sunday when the ATVs had gone, she headed out for a walk in the forest, using the entrance, loosely speaking, at the bottom of the hill because Frankie was at his cabin, getting ready for deer season, or duck season, or mastodon season, and although she had the legal right to use the road past his cabin, she wasn't in the mood for a confrontation. If he *was* preparing for deer season, or duck season, he'd be cleaning his rifles.

And she saw right there, just ten feet off the road and just two feet to the left of the path, four huge near-bursting bags of garbage. What the fuck. Seriously?

She carried them back where they belonged. To Bullert's property. Specifically, into Bullert's screened porch.

The bears did their thing. The raccoons did their thing. There was a lovely mess to clean up when they arrived the following Friday.

And the hardware store was, oddly enough, all out of screen.

Right in the middle of blackfly season.

One full-moon midnight, when *finally*, finally, everyone, *everyone*, had shut up, and she could take off her headphones and take out her earplugs, she headed down to the water, sighing with anticipation as she settled into her chair to stare out at the moonlight glimmering on the water and—a runway? What the hell?

Across the lake, the people from Windsor had apparently just put up a bunch of lights in front of their cottage, two rows in fact, presumably marking a path to the lake. And forgotten to turn them off.

So she walked over the next day—it would be weeks before they came up again—to turn them off. And discovered they were solar lights. That didn't have an on-off switch. Whose bright idea was that? So now she was supposed to see an airport runway of lights whenever she looked out across the lake—every night, all night, for the rest of her life? Lights that served no purpose whatsoever? (Because, hello, no one was there.)

If we lived in the city, she thought, maybe it wouldn't be so bad; they'd get lost in the context. But we live on a lake in a forest. Where the stars are amazing and the moon gleams and glimmers across the water. And now there were a dozen lights at eye level a little to her left whenever she looked out across that lovely dark water. They stood out like a middle finger.

She called the woman that night, around one o'clock in the morning, after her break, during which she always went for a walk with Shiggles, to tell her that one of her lights had fallen over, so if she was planning on walking from her cottage door to the lake, to be careful. After all, it was a good twenty feet on a ten degree slope.

The woman replied, in the voice you use when you speak to a ten-year-old, "I'm not planning to walk down to the lake tonight."

"Oh," Vic replied then, with the perfect sense of a four-year-old, "then why didn't you turn off your lights when you left?"

"They're solar lights. They don't turn on and off."

"Then you should've bought the kind that *does* turn off," her inner four-year-old said. "Or you could cover them up when you leave," she said helpfully.

"Or here's a thought," her inner bitch took over, "there's a thing that gives you light exactly and only when and where you need it. It's called a flashlight."

True, using a flashlight wouldn't provide the decorative effect. (They're actually *called* 'decorative'—by the aesthetically-challenged business graduates now working in marketing departments.) But if a light is on in the middle of a forest and you don't see it, is it still decorative?

She called the woman again the next night, at two o'clock in the morning, to tell her that another one had fallen over.

Does she think the lights keep the wildlife away? A motion-sensor light would do that just as well. Better, actually, because of its startle effect.

The following night, she didn't get back from her night walk until three o'clock. "Hi, it's me again. Just calling to let you know that *another* one of your lights fell over..."

The following weekend, at four o'clock, shortly after she went to bed, someone's car alarm went off. Again. A bat probably flew too close to the Taylors' Caravan. Again. Or maybe a raccoon wandered too close to the Levines' Caravan. Again.

It was ten minutes before whosever car it was woke up, figured out it was their car, got out of bed, put on a robe, couldn't find shoes, found a flashlight—they're the one cottage with*out* solar lights—went out, and dealt with it.

So the weekend after that, when she was out on her coffee break walk, around midnight, she stopped twenty feet from one of the Caravans and upended a bag into which she'd scraped bacon-grease-covered-grass, collected the previous Sunday from near the back door of the other Caravan owners. By the time she got back to her place, she heard the alarm.

Ten minutes after that, the scream.

Apparently Bullert got his little boy every third weekend, so one weekend in mid-June, about five minutes after his pick-up truck roared in, a little kid, couldn't've been more than six years old, started zooming up and down the lane on a little dirt bike. She didn't know they made them that small. Dirt bikes, that is.

First of all, she thought, there's just something wrong with a kid that young having a dirt bike. What ever happened to real bikes? Bicycles. And people wonder why our kids are either hyperactive or obese. Or both.

Second of all, there's something *very* wrong with a kid driving a dirt bike up and down, and up and down, and up and down, and up and down, and up and down, and up and down a lane on which there are now four permanent residents and eight seasonal residents. (Two built on lots that, again, she didn't even know *were* lots—she'd thought the one bit of land was part of the Johnsons' property and the other bit part of the Campbells' property. Who the hell approved such small lots on a lake? Once all the lots were developed, they'd be as sardined as they would be in the city.)

Which meant the kid was annoying the fuck out of a significant number of people.

So she went out to tell him so. She was ready to go for a walk anyway.

Next thing she knew his dad, Bullert, came charging up the lane on his ATV to confront her.

"You don't own the fucking road!" he screamed at her, his 'God's Gift to the World' tshirt barely covered his distended belly.

"Neither do you!" she screamed back. Instead of pointing out that there were two competing notions of public property—no one owns it, so everyone can do what they want on it (his); we all own it, so we all have to share it (hers)—and that hers was better than his.

Maybe he didn't know it when he bought the place, but given his ATVing since, he surely knew now that there were several stretches of road, nearby, that didn't have *any* houses, stretches of road where the kid could ride up and down ad infinitum with much less annoyance.

In fact, she pointed out, there was just such a road around the corner parallel to the lane, ending just two lots down from his house. She was referring, of course, to Campbell's road.

Why was there a road parallel to the lane that went to the same place—the Campbells' house? This is why. When Vic bought her place, the lane wasn't maintained by the Township. That meant that it didn't get plowed in the winter. Some days she had to shovel her way to the corner. About a hundred feet. Most days, since Dave (Campbell) had to leave for work before her, he plowed it. Understandably, he was getting sick and tired of doing it and wanted the Township to take over. But they wouldn't do that until the lane was widened. So he asked all of them (Vic, the Johnsons, and the four seasonals) if they would each pitch in $1,000 to have that done. Vic was the only one to say 'Sure'. (Actually, since she didn't have $1,000, she offered instead $1,000 worth of piano lessons for their kids.) So, in a supreme 'Fuck you' gesture—because why should they alone pay for it when everyone on the lane would benefit from it—the Campbells put in a whole new road to their place. Pretty much parallel to the existing road.

Point is, there wasn't anyone living on that road. Campbell's road. So, Vic reasoned, why couldn't the kid zoom up and down, and up and down, and up and down, and up and down, and up and down *that* road? Sure, they'd still hear it, but it wouldn't be *quite* as annoying.

Plus, though this really wasn't a point in favour as far as she was concerned, the kid would be less likely to be hit by one of them backing out of their driveway.

"You don't own the fucking road!" Bullert screamed at her again, getting off his ATV and standing closer to her than she would like.

"*You* shouldn't even be *walking* on the road. It's a *road*!"

And to prove his point, from then on, every time he passed her and Shiggles in his pick-up, he sped up, showering them in dust and gravel.

One time, he even drove straight for them. She didn't know it, since she was facing away, in order not to get gravel in her face, standing over Shiggles at the edge of the road as far as they could get without actually going down into the ditch. When he passed them, she felt a swoosh of air and realized only then that he'd come within about six inches. If she'd happened to crouch down to retie her shoelace or, more likely, to get a safe grip on Shiggles, her hip would've been clipped by his bumper and she could've been spending the rest of her life in a wheelchair.

Asshole.

Next thing she knew, the kid was zooming up and down the little trail that went through the crown land adjacent to her cabin, the one that led to the spring.

And then he discovered the half-overgrown driveway of the empty lot on the other side of her.

So he was doing a horseshoe around her, down the left side to the water and back, then onto the road behind her, then down the right side to the water and back. Over and over and over and over and over.

She was sure his dad had told him to.

So she stopped him. The kid. She asked him if he knew how much the sound of his dirt bike irritated her, how she couldn't read or do any work when he did what he was doing.

"Yeah," he said in his little six-year-old voice.

"Then why are you doing it?" she asked, encouragingly. Children are our future.

"BECAUSE YOU'RE A FUCKING CUNT!" he screamed, then took off.

All right then.

She could've put up a 'No Trespassing' sign, but it would've been an eyesore. And she wasn't sure either of them could read.

She could've set some boulders across, but the kid probably would've made his way between or around them.

The only thing to do, she thought, is cut down one of the trees at the road's edge so it would lay across the path. Trees were always falling down, so it wouldn't seem terribly odd. In fact, she saw that there was one in exactly the right place, already half gone. It was a thin one with lots of branches, which would do just fine.

She went to her shed to get her chainsaw.

Right. Like she had a chainsaw. She didn't even have a lawnmower. Whenever she felt the need to cut her grass, she just told herself to wait a couple months and it would all be dead.

She went to her shed to get her axe.

Well. She wasn't a lumberjack. (And it should be clear by now that she wasn't okay.)

So when she gave the tree a good thwack, it fell—across the lane.

Just as the kid was zooming up it for the 123rd time.

If he'd been travelling under the speed limit—whatever that is for six-year-olds on dirt bikes—he might've been able to stop in time. Especially if he'd been facing the front.

The bike hit the tree and he went flying.

Dead on impact. She did check.

She carried on with her task and managed to drag the tree off the road and across the path. Not sure it mattered much now.

By the time the guy realized his kid was missing, the wolves had come and carried him off, probably just as pissed at the ATVs and dirt bikes.

His wife was pissed too, when he returned without the kid. He protested that he'd forgotten he'd had him that weekend. Like that made it better.

By late June, it became clear that Bullert and his buddies were into the whole campfire-at-night thing. Well, actually, she suspected it was more the get-drunk-and-make-like-an-asshole thing, but in any case, every time they were up, they'd get a good fire going just before dark. And for about six hours, everyone on Paradise Lake would hear their shouted and hollered conversation. Shouted and hollered so they could hear each other above the radio they had on.

The 'conversation' typically went something like "He was a fucking idiot and I fucking told him to leave it the fuck alone but he's a fuckin asshole eh, so he beat the fucking shit out of it which was fucking hilarious because the guy's such a fuckwad..."

She wasn't averse to the word herself, but she tended to use it only for extreme frustration or extreme rage.

The woman in the cottage next to Bullert's, Mrs. Archer, was the kind of person who winced every time she heard the word. By the end of her first weekend up, she had a full-time nervous tic going on in her eyelid.

By the end of their second weekend, she and her husband had put their cottage up for sale.

On their third weekend, Bullert and his buddies realized they could move their tv outside. They could watch the game down at the water while they had their campfire.

The Archers lowered their asking price.

And the weekend after that, Bullert and his buddies showed up with two trailers of jetslams.

For those of you who haven't had the pleasure, jetslams have a very special whine. It's engineered to take the enamel off your teeth. And the way Bullert and his buddies drove them—

The lake is small, this has been said already. You could get across it in a jetslam in about ten seconds.

Which means that in a minute you could go back and forth and back and forth and back and forth.

Or you could go up and down and up down and up and down.

Or you could go around and around and around and around, jumping your own wake.

Or you could zig zag, pretending you were doing a slalom course.

If there were four jetslams on the lake at the same time, all four things could be done pretty much at once.

And the lake is surrounded by forested hills, that has also been said already. So imagine four jetslams tearing around in a cave on a small pool of water.

Imagine a dozen people living in that cave.

Since several of those people were hard of hearing and/or spent most of their lives inside with the windows closed watching their flat-screen tv with the volume on high, they weren't too bothered.

The Archers were not such people. They lowered their asking price even more.

Vic also was not such a person.

Just for comparison, various sound charts put city traffic at around 80dB, the subway at 88dB, a garbage truck at 100dB. Two-stroke engines—chainsaws, boat motors, dirt bikes, ATVs, PWCs—are around 110dB. So living on Paradise Lake had become worse than living in the city.

Much worse, because the decibel is a logarithmic unit: an increase in 10dB means *it sounds ten times as loud.*

Furthermore, the World Health Organization says 55 dB is "highly annoying" to most of us. Continuous exposure to noise 40-70dB can affect a person's hearing. Hearing protection is recommended even for occasional sounds of 85dB.

Vic had a semi-basement in which she could hunker down for the duration. (There was something about where she was, perhaps it was her location at the end of a cove, that meant that being inside with the windows closed and the tv on wasn't quite enough.) (She supposed that if she added earplugs to the mix, that might do it. But, seriously, on a beautiful summer day? When the bugs are finally gone?)

The other option was to just not be there.

So most weekends she just kayaked away from it all to the other end of the lake.

Thing is, if she wasn't gone by the time they started, she was screwed. Apparently it was sport for jetslammers to run circles around kayakers.

First time that happened, she already had her earplugs in and her headphones on. (Unfortunately, wearing earplugs meant she wouldn't be able to hear the baby loons learn to call. They made the cutest little toot-toot sounds. Oh wait a minute. There probably wouldn't *be* any more baby loons.)

And by this time, she also had a charcoal-lined respirator with her at all times to keep the fumes out of her brain.

There was no real danger of tipping, and Shiggles knew to scramble off her perch on the prow and snuggle between her knees, to be gripped tight.

Still, it pissed her off.

So as she paddled past Bullert's dock on her way home that evening, she asked them not to do that again, please.

"You don't own the fucking lake!" was his response.

To prove it, five seconds after she'd docked her kayak, he

roared into the cove and did circles in front of her dockraft for a good half hour.

She got the message. (*He* owned the lake.)

In what other context, she asked herself, are motorized vehicles allowed to travel at high speeds in a random fashion? Cars and motorcycles are required to drive on roads, in prescribed lanes even. ATVs and dirt bikes have to stay on the trails. Planes are required to log their flight plan and stick to it. Ships? There are shipping lanes, are there not? But motor boats? And jetslams in particular? They can zig zag, go in circles, turn right, turn left—and there's no way to anticipate where they'll go next. They don't have blinkers. They can speed up, slow down, come to a standstill in the middle of wherever, make a U-turn—

She had once stopped before she crossed from the lake per se to the river, the only spot where she couldn't hug the shoreline, to wait until two jetslams had zoomed by. When she was one-quarter of the way across, they suddenly turned back. She too turned back and paddled for her life.

Literally. As she discovered the next day when she did a bit of reading.

Apparently there had been a great many injuries and a great many deaths by jetslams. Apparently it was the jet stream that provided the steering capability. So if a jetslam was heading straight for something, or someone, and the driver cut the throttle, he (it's almost always a he) would lose his steering, and so run right into the something. Or someone. At a slightly slower speed, true, but still. Whatever he'd run into would get mangled. Or killed.

Because not only do jetslams not have off-throttle steering, they don't have brakes.

Something else she discovered as a result of her reading was that there had been many attempts to get jetslams banned. The American Canoe Association had prepared a 52-page report over ten years prior, detailing the damage they do to the water, to the wildlife, to the shoreline, and so on. The report had apparently made no difference. The jetslam manufacturers had probably gotten involved.

In Canada, a bill was introduced by Senator Mira Spivak in 2001: Bill S-26, *The Personal Watercraft Act,* would simply enable communities to restrict the use of jetslams if they so desired, much as they can now set speed limits or restrict waterskiing on their lakes. The bill did not make it through into law. It became Bill S-10 on a second try in 2003. In 2008, parliament was still debating the bill, which had by then become S-221. It was voted on again in 2010, and again not passed. (Spivak had retired in 2009; she was seventy-five and presumably had had enough.)

So at that point, Vic realized that just being pissed off by the jetslammers' behaviour was naïve.

And she hated being naïve.

TurboJetslams

Monday. Monday was beautiful. Still. Beyond calm. Even the trees were holding their breath. Which was actually not a good thing, Vic thought to herself, because we really need the oxygen they exhale. And we really need them to inhale gobs and gobs of carbon dioxide.

Correction. Monday *morning* was beautiful. Because after the weekend, once everyone who actually lived on the lake came back from wherever they'd escaped to—most went to visit their kids, see the grandkids; some just hid inside all weekend, drinking themselves numb in front of the tv—they'd resume their lives.

On Monday afternoon, they'd cut the grass.

Tuesday, they'd trim the weeds.

Wednesday, they'd chainsaw some wood.

Thursday, they'd test their generators.

It was a Thursday that she went into town. Both libraries were open on Thursdays.

On her way back, she saw that the Township had put up a new sign at the boundary road. "Welcome to Your Summer Playground!"

Great. Thanks a lot.

At the end of July, someone bought the Archers' place.

Correction. Three someones.

The new little sign at their driveway said:

The Sinclairs!
John and Liz – Billy, Bobby, Susie
Bill and Sue – Jim, Jade, Junior, Jeni
Ed and Trish – Tammi, Trixie, Riley, Dane

It was a three-family purchase. Vic figured each would have two weeks' vacation. There went pretty much the whole summer.

Turned out she was wrong. Two of them had three weeks, so usually there were two families there at once. It was the Taylors and the Levines times ten. Plus Bullert's crew.

Because the Sinclairs were also jetslam addicts. Every one of them. Even the eight-year-olds. Between the Sinclairs and Bullert's crew, there were six machines.

Oh well, she thought hopefully, maybe several head-on collisions would ensue. Natural selection at work.

What did ensue was the woman on the other side of the Bullerts got hit when she was out swimming. What she was doing swimming when the jetslams were out, Vic had no idea. The woman was a good five feet from her dock, wore a full red bathing suit, and had one of those bright orange traffic cones on her head.

About those little signs at people's driveways. And on the tree at the intersection of Paradise Lake Lane and Campbell's Road. And on the tree at the turn-off from the main road. "The Levines", "The Taylors", "Jill and Dill", "Fred's Fishing Central"— What was it with that?

Did they do that in the city? Put a sign at the corner with their name on it and an arrow so people know where they live?

Of course not.

So why did they do it here?

Because they're deluded, Vic answered her own question. They think that when they're here, they're away from civilization, they're in the wild. Perhaps, she thought, it's all this forest that makes them think that. And the gravel roads, the absence of stores and street lights. The little name signs maintain that delusion.

Problem is, when they leave civilization behind, they apparently leave civility behind as well. Tossing their garbage, wrecking the roads, turning up their radios, moving their tvs outside—it was all part of the same thing: we're here all alone in the middle of nowhere, so we can damn well do whatever we want!

And the supposed lack of civilization didn't bring out just the anarchist, it brought out the pioneer. That explained the sudden obsession with building things. Cottages, bunkies, docks, rafts, birdhouses. Guys who'd never pick up a hammer in the city were suddenly building multi-split-levels. With their own two hands.

Worse, it brought out the primeval. (Or maybe men's brains had never progressed past the primeval.) And that explained the need to roar. With ATVs, dirt bikes, jetslams—

Which also explained why everyone's IQ dropped fifty points to Neanderthal level when they got here.

And, she suddenly understood, pioneer plus primeval equalled power tools.

This realization hit her like a 15-amp 12-inch dual bevel compound miter saw when she was online one day trying to identify a new sound, very unlike a series of three bright notes followed by a melodic warble, and found a page titled "Manly Power Tools" at askmen.com, which said: "In 1895, German inventor Wilhelm Emil Fein developed the first electric hand drill, marking the beginning of man's love affair with power tools. We like them because they're powerful, noisy, and enable us to destroy almost anything with relative ease. However, they also allow us to build something with that same ease and earsplitting noise. A good collection of power tools may be the last remaining mark of a true man. The whir of a circular saw tells your neighbor that you're not f*cking around—you're a guy who knows what he's doing. And make no mistake, women love to watch us work with power tools."

What? What?!

Clearly the marketing departments at all the big box hardware and building supply stores had bought into this shit.

So back before power lawn mowers were invented and people used manual lawnmowers, before string trimmers were invented and people used clippers, before leafblowers were invented and people used rakes, before power tools of all kinds were invented and people used hammers, screwdrivers, and sandpaper—men weren't manly men. And—

Ah! That's why whenever she'd asked a man to limit his noise, he'd not only not acceded to her request, he'd escalated his noise-making and/or responded with confrontational aggression! Not only was she a woman asking a man to do something, and most men would rather die than be seen doing something a woman had asked him to do—would rather kill, really, said woman—she was also essentially asking them to castrate themselves.

But of course they're not. Away from civilization. In the wild. Here all alone in the middle of nowhere. They're here in the middle of someone's neighbourhood.

So you want your friends and relatives to be able to find you when they come visit? Here's an idea. Give them your address. You live at 26 Poplar Lane.

By the end of the Sinclairs' first weekend, she discovered that at least one of them was a heavy smoker. There were ten butts on the lane. She picked them up and dumped them on their porch.

She did it again the following Monday.

And again the next Monday.

Then she gave up—you know what they say about the definition of insanity—and just scuffed a hole in the dirt with her heel and buried them, one by one. Took her several minutes, but then for the rest of the week when she walked down the lane, she wasn't seeing cigarette butts every few feet.

By early August, the loons had disappeared. She didn't know if they'd left the lake or had been killed. Apparently it was sport to run over them. They can't dive if they've got a baby on board.

TurboJetslams

Since she was spending so much time on the lake, she couldn't help but notice the sudden proliferation of Canadian flags flying on people's properties, lakeside. She didn't understand why everyone had suddenly become so very patriotic. As far as she knew, Canada was still a low achiever, an underperformer, a disgrace, actually.

We're the second worst of all the industrialized countries when it comes to sulfur dioxide emissions, she said to herself as she paddled past one of the forementioned flags, the second worst when it comes to carbon monoxide emissions, and the second worst when it comes to greenhouse gas emissions (we pump out 48% more greenhouse gas emissions per capita than the OECD average, up about 13% since 1990, in violation of our international commitments); we're also the second worst with regard to water consumption, the second worst when it comes to energy efficiency, the third worst when it comes to energy consumption, and fourth worst when it comes to producing ozone-depleting stuff. In short, we're responsible for the floods, the droughts, the famines, the hurricanes, the tornadoes. (So why isn't everyone screaming at us, and the U.S., 'You broke it, you fix it!')

Turning our attention away from the environment, she continued her lecture, to no one, we're barely in the top quarter when it comes to the gender gap in wages, political power (Rwanda, Senegal, South Africa, Mozambique, Costa Rica, Uganda, Angola, Nepal,

Serbia, Slovenia, Ethiopia, and Mexico have more women in their parliaments than Canada does), and health (it's safer to be pregnant in Estonia than in Canada). Speaking of which, we're one of the last six countries in the developed world not to have paternity leave. And we're apparently unable to produce even one female Nobel prize winner (every single one of Canada's 21 Nobel Laureates have been men).

So, Vic wondered, why in god's name are so many people letting the world know (well, letting other Canadians know) that they're Canadian?

Because they're not, she realized after a moment's thought. They've mistaken the national flag for a claim stake, for the thing you stick in the ground when you want to say, 'This is mine!' (We're back to the regression thing—the pioneer thing, the primeval thing...)

Either that or one of the manly men stores had them on sale one weekend.

One Friday—she'd taken to leaving her house by three o'clock on Fridays because as soon as the Bullert crew and the Sinclairs arrived, they'd rev up their dirt bikes, ATVs, and/or jetslams and spend the next hour or two raising everybody's blood pressure. It was their way of relieving the stress of the drive up.

One Friday, on her way back after dark, she noticed that that there was a different bunch of people at the cottage on the right, a few up from Tim and Lyle, than there had been the weekend before.

Oh god. The owner was using it as a rental.

The problem with rentals is that they were even worse than the regular weekenders. They figured they'd paid their thousand bucks, so they had a right to do whatever they want. (Actually, maybe they weren't so different from the regular weekenders...) It was an overgeneralization of rights if she ever saw one.

As soon as she'd rounded the last corner, she'd heard THUMP THUMP THUMP woody woody THUMP THUMP THUMP woody woody THUMP THUMP THUMP woody woody THUMP THUMP. All she heard was the drums. THUMP THUMP THUMP woody woody THUMP THUMP THUMP woody woody THUMP THUMP THUMP woody woody THUMP THUMP. She didn't know if it was heavy metal, country, or hiphop. THUMP THUMP THUMP woody woody THUMP THUMP THUMP woody woody THUMP THUMP THUMP woody woody THUMP THUMP. And she really didn't care.

She waited until Monday. No point in doing anything over the weekend. That afternoon—THUMP THUMP THUMP woody woody THUMP THUMP THUMP woody woody THUMP THUMP THUMP woody woody THUMP THUMP—she left Shiggles at home, took her kayak drybag of essentials, walked over to the Levine's place (they weren't there that week), and borrowed their blue kayak.

She paddled out from behind the peninsula to the dock of the rental cottage. There was only one guy there; the rest of his friends must have gone into town for a beer run.

"Thanks, but no thanks," she said.

He looked at her like she was the idiot.

"You're offering to share your music with me," she explained, nodding to the super-sized retro boom box he had sitting on the dock, "but I don't want to listen to it. So no thanks."

"I wasn't offering to share," he spat into the water. Eew.

"Oh. So you're *forcing* me to listen to it? Why?"

"I'm not forcing you."

"Well, yeah, you are. I can hear it from my place. Can't really close my ears, can I."

"So go inside."

"No *you* go inside." Why is the default unlimited noise? "Or just turn it down, so only you can hear it."

"I like it loud."

"Then use earbuds. Or headphones. It's win-win. You get to listen to the music you want to listen to, as loud as you want, and I get to sit outside and *not* listen to music I don't want to listen to." It was too much. She'd realized that halfway through. "If you use earbuds or headphones, we both get what we want," she provided the *Coles Notes* version.

Silence. Or stupefaction.

"You're not going to turn it down, are you."

"Duh."

"You think you have the right to force me to do something I don't want to do. When I'm at home. On my own property. You think you have the right to trespass?"

"I'm not trespassing."

"The sound from your boom box is." Have people no ability to consider the invisible, the intangible? "You may as well be throwing paint onto my property. Or pouring smoke from a pile of burning tires through my window." Oh god, don't give him any ideas. Actually— She tucked that second idea away for later consideration.

He stared at her. His sense of entitlement was truly—bewildering.

So she paddled out of reach. Then calmly put in her earplugs, put on her headphones, connected them to her iPod, and selected her *Zen of Sky* album.

Then she pulled out her bear alarm. Actually, it was a Sports Paal—you can get them on eBay. What it is is a small box, the size of a measuring tape, with a pin in it like a grenade. Pull out the pin and it emits an ear-splitting high frequency tone intended to alert passers-by to an assault. Or, in her case, in the event Shiggles engages with a bear, to frighten the bear into running away.

The guy involuntarily put his hands over his ears, then cursed at her from here to hell and back. Or so she assumed. She wasn't very good at reading lips.

Then he stood up and dove in, straight for her. Oh please. Like she couldn't paddle faster than he could swim.

Once he heaved himself back onto the dock, he turned and called her a kun. No, that must've been cunt.

He tried to turn up the volume on his boom box, but discovered that he'd already had it as loud as it could go. She could've told him that.

Then he sat back down belligerently, apparently having decided to outlast her. Or the alarm.

Turns out Energizer batteries *do* keep going and going...

A mere five minutes later, he headed up to the cottage, leaving the boom box there at full volume just to spite her. She paddled to the dock, turned it off, confiscated it, put the pin back into her bear alarm, and paddled away.

He watched her disappear behind the peninsula.

And when the Levines came up the next weekend, they were surprised, and confused, to discover that someone had sunk their pretty blue kayak.

Something else about rentals was that often there was hollering well into the night. Oddly enough, both the Levines and the Taylors thought that that was totally inappropriate. They actually made a point of saying so to Vic the next time they saw her. (Why they thought she was the designated do-something-about-it person, she had no idea.)

"But it's no different than the hollering your kids do during the day," she said.

"But it's at night," Sara or Sura or something replied.

"Your point?" Vic asked. "They're equally annoying, equally a trespass. Everyone should keep their noise on their own property."

"But people sleep at night," the woman explained.

"Actually," Vic said, "there are half a dozen people here who nap in the afternoon. Haven't you met *any* of your neighbours?"

Of course Sara or Sura or something hadn't. That would be

admitting it *was* a neighbourhood.

"And," Vic continued, "it's incorrect to assume that sleep needs more quiet than other activities that I, for one, might do during the day."

She thought Sara, or Sura, or something, had trouble grasping that. Reading and writing, let alone thinking deeply, were not activities on her radar.

"Certainly it's not more important," Vic added.

One day when she and Shiggles were out walking on the road, the Taylors' car passed them, and she noticed that a kid was at the wheel in dad's lap.

Great idea! That's *exactly* what we need! Eight-year-olds behind the wheel.

Granted, men are worse drivers than women (just ask the insurance companies) and so need more practice, but, she thought to herself, this would just encourage them, condition them, to think of motorized vehicles as toys and tokens of manhood.

She remembered that her iPod—she'd taken to putting it in her pocket, along with earbuds, when she went for a walk in case the backhoe started up when she was within hearing distance but still miles from home, and her earplugs and headphones—had a built-in camera, so she was ready for them on their way back. She stood in the middle of the road, made sure the licence plate was in the frame, and in focus, then smiled and waved.

Idiots, they both waved back.

She took the shot.

And somehow the OPP got hold of it.

Once the Millers had finished their interior decorating, they turned their attention back to the outside. Specifically, to the peninsula.

Vic had reconciled herself to the inevitable, the permanent presence of the aluminum boat glinting in the sun (she assumed they hadn't noticed the fridge) (how can you not notice a bright, stainless steel fridge sitting right outside your window?), and had done some exterior decorating herself, affixing another bunch of branches to another tree like she had to block the view of the Taylors' red roof. So she couldn't see the boat from her couch.

She also went to a garden center and bought a largish cedar tree, left it in its pot, and put it on her dockraft just so. Her view of the boat was blocked from there as well.

While she was at the garden center, she'd also bought half a dozen little cedar trees. Planted them down on the peninsula one day when the Millers weren't home. She figured they wouldn't notice. She was right.

It would be a good ten years before the trees were tall enough and thick enough to act as an acoustic and visual screen, but maybe she'd still be alive. And not yet deaf and blind.

But mid-July, a red canoe showed up beside the aluminum boat.

She bought another tree from the garden center.

Then a dock.

And another tree.

Then one of those put-it-together-yourself gazebos.

Two other trees.

Then a paddle boat and a waterski boat. And a second dock.

She had trees lined up along the entire eight-foot edge of her dockraft. She had no space left.

Then they bought one of those blow-up rafts, in bright yellow. It bobbed in the water. All day, catching her eye.

If all this shit truly made them happy, if their kids couldn't wait to go down to the water and play, well, that would be one thing. But they hardly ever used any of it.

So while on the one hand, she was very, very glad of that (she had to hear them only Saturday and Sunday afternoons), on the other hand, they'd taken away, completely and permanently, something so incredibly precious to her—for nothing. Most of the time, they didn't care about their aluminum boat, their canoe, their gazebo, their paddle boat, their waterski boat, or their bright yellow blow-up raft bobbing away. Half the time, she was sure they forgot they even had all that shit.

Speaking of which, how was it they *had* all that shit? The guy drove a truck for the local logging company. Obviously, she thought, it was time to toss out the idea that unskilled labour is the lower class. Like Bullert, who also had just a high school education (maybe not even that), Miller had a new pickup. They weren't cheap. About $40,000. Her used Saturn cost $9,000.

Their trucks got about 15 mpg. Her Saturn got about 40 mpg. And gas wasn't cheap.

Add the canoe, the waterski boat, the paddle boat, the ATVs, the dirt bikes, the jetslams—it had to add up to almost $100,000. She had a kayak and a laptop. $1,000.

Oh but they couldn't afford to send their kids to university. (She didn't have kids. Wouldn't've been able to afford them.) (Well, that and she hated them.)

And they were in debt, eh, because they didn't have one of them high-paying jobs, so give 'em a break! Right. The local plumber charged an hourly rate twice what she'd been paid as a university instructor.

Some time in August, a plane showed up. It was big, it was white, and it was tied to one of the few remaining trees across from her. In the once pretty little cove.

Apparently Jim owned a seaplane he'd been keeping at the nearby airport. And apparently he'd decided to keep it in the cove instead. In the once pretty little cove.

And again, he never used it. (Actually, that's not true. He did use it once. And everyone on the lake rushed out of their houses thinking surely a Boeing 707 was about to crash land. What a noise! Amplified of course, as sounds are on Paradise Lake. Vic grabbed her earplugs. Everyone else put their hands over their ears. People who happened to be on the lake put their motors into high gear to get out of the way. Ducks and loons dove for their lives.)

Given such sporadic use, why couldn't he just drive his little aluminum boat to the end of the lake and up the river to the airport's launch whenever he wanted to go flying? He wouldn't even have to drive around, now that he lived on the lake.

Vic stared across at the plane. Could she build an extension to her dockraft? A long, curving walkway—what do you call it, an isthmus? a jetty?—and put trees all along it? She'd still have a small bit of forest and lake to look at. If she turned her chair away from the lake altogether and just faced the end by the spring.

But even if she could do that, there was no way she could not see the plane from her deck, her porch, her desk, her couch—she may as well live in an apartment in the city overlooking a parking lot.

The damn thing was sitting in, completely filling, his half of the cove. Though...technically...he didn't actually own his half of the cove—he didn't own the water his plane was sitting in. Hm.

Turns out she never had to build the isthmus. Or jetty. Whatever.

Because somehow, in the middle of the night, the plane came loose. It bumped into the yellow raft, puncturing it, then drifted clear around the peninsula and crashed into the Taylors' party barge. Did a fair bit of damage. Mutual damage.

Woohoo, she applauded herself. A twofer!

The following week, a trailer appeared on a piece of land mid-way up the lane. Again, Vic had thought the land in question was part of the lots on either side, not a separate lot.

The appearance of the trailer meant that within two years (the Township did have one bylaw), a cottage would be built. She hoped they'd hire the local construction crew. It would be done in three weeks, Monday to Friday, nine to five. If they did it themselves, there'd be no telling how many years it would take.

It also meant that, in the meantime, they'd have to pay just $200 a year in property taxes instead of something closer to $2,000. Even though they'd use the roads, the dump, the library—scratch that, what was she thinking—even though they'd use the roads and the dump just as much. More, probably. (Unless, of course, they opted for hosting Teddy Bear Picnics.)

And since they probably wouldn't pay to hook up to hydro until they started building, it meant that everyone on Paradise Lake would hear their generator whenever they wanted to watch tv. They'd probably also hear their tv, given how loud it would have to be to be audible over the generator.

When she paddled past, on her way up the river, she saw that the teenaged son was up with all of his friends. Three tents were set up around the trailer.

She thought for a minute. Had she seen an outhouse? Or would there be shitting in the bush. Ten feet from the lake.

She heard a belch. A long, extended belch.

A lot of shitting in the bush.

She considered giving a heads-up to the woman down-current with the red bathing suit who swam every day. Scratch that. Used to swim every day.

She thought nothing more of them until well after she'd returned. Until two o'clock in the morning, in fact. At which time the bongo drums started.

They probably have a fire too, she thought, as she set aside her work and headed out.

It was that whole primeval thing again. Sitting by a fire, sending messages by drum, chowing down on a mammoth— What's next, she wondered as she got to their driveway, hurling spears?

Something whizzed by, just missing her face.

"What the fuck?" she screamed as she dove into the bush at the end of their driveway

"Sorry!" How he'd heard her, given the bongos, she had no idea.

She picked herself up and walked in.

They had one of those straw targets set up on the driveway halfway in. Its back to the road. See what she meant by the drop in IQ?

It was, she noticed, as yet unpunctured.

"Give me that thing," she said to the nearest twenty-something, the one with the bow and arrow in his hand. He handed it over. She loaded the arrow and fired it into his foot.

"Fuck!" he started hopping.

"And enough with the bongos!" she screamed.

They stared at her.

"There's a fire ban," she said then, searching for the one in charge. The one with half a brain.

"What's a fire ban?" someone asked.

What? What?!

"We haven't had rain for over two weeks," she explained. "No outdoor fires are allowed."

She waited for it. Altogether now, 'We can do whatever we want on our own property!'

Surprisingly enough, they were silent. Probably still trying to figure out the relevance of rain to fires.

"Suppose that thing," she pointed to the six-foot high blaze, "throws a spark." She bent down, picked up a rock, and tossed it into the fire. Some of those present—not all, note—moved back from the shower of sparks.

Unfortunately, one of the sparks landed on one of the tents. Nylon, it blazed immediately.

Shit. She looked around, but they didn't have buckets of water at the ready. Of course not.

"Call 911!" she screamed. Her cabin was just five lots away.

"AND ENOUGH WITH THE BONGOS!"

But as quickly as it had blazed, the tent, now an ex-tent, had congealed into a sad, melted marshmallow. A sad, melted *blue* marshmallow.

"Never mind."

Or maybe it's the trailer and campfire that misleads them, she thought as she walked back to her place. It makes them think they're in some public campground instead of someone's neighbourhood. Because would they sit in their back yard at home and play the bongo drums at two o'clock in the morning? She thought not.

But even in a campground, there are rules about this sort of thing. There are even wardens who walk around enforcing those rules.

Which means it would be quieter there than here, she realized.

And thought about getting a second kayak and a roof rack.

Some time after, late one morning, she made her way down to the water with her cup of tea and her work-in-progress. Hearing the jetslammers already at it, she immediately put in her earplugs, then reached for her headphones and CD player—what the hell? The lake looked like it had developed the plague. It was covered with ugly white bleach bottle blisters. There must have been fifty of them.

She found out that afternoon that the Sinclairs had spent the morning attaching one bleach bottle to every deadhead. They'd wanted to make the lake safe.

The day before, one of them had been jumping the wake of a

boat towing a kid on waterskis. Back and forth, back and forth, getting higher and higher, oh what fun— The waterskiing kid fell. The jetslammer drove right over him. Frankly, she hadn't been sure they'd noticed at the end of the day that they were missing a kid. That's probably why they had so many.

In any case, it had nothing to do with the submerged logs. Now marked by ugly white bleach bottles.

So…they disappeared one night. One long night.

In the process, the logs became a little less submerged. Oops.

Next morning, she made her way down to the water with her cup of tea and a bunch of Bristol board signs she'd prepared.

Gentlemen, start your engines.

Did they think that since the bleach bottles were gone, so were the deadheads? Who knows.

The first guy to hit one was ejected in a most spectacular fashion. Remember that opening clip from the *Wide World of Sports*? That ski jumper soaring like he was shot out of a cannon—then flipping over and over and over again like a ragdoll before finally coming to rest? Like that. She rifled through her Bristol boards and held up a '10'.

By mid-afternoon, the screaming kids were in high gear, despite the morning's fatalities, so she went out in her kayak. Once she was out of earshot, it was beautiful. Until someone decided to go fishing.

If they had just started up their motor, puttered from their dock to a spot, then turned off their motor, and sat there fishing, that would've been okay.

It would've been even more okay if they'd gotten from their dock to their fishing spot with one of those silent electric motors.

But usually, Vic knew by now, one of three other things would happen.

The guy—yes, it was, again, invariably a man—would putter around the entire perimeter of the lake, taking a good hour to do so and sounding exactly like one of those loud gas generators, with his fishing line dragging out the back of the boat. Because he was just too weak to cast and reel in more than once or twice.

Or he would putter along behind or beside her. That way she got to hear the motor even through her earplugs and headphones.

And if he puttered along ahead of her, she also got the benefit of his fumes, which, as previously explained, would ensure that she'd have a full-blown headache by the time she got home. Because, alas, her charcoal respirator wasn't quite up to the task. And the gas mask she'd ordered hadn't yet arrived.

Once, since these guys didn't move any faster than she paddled, she just pulled over for fifteen minutes to let the obnoxiousness get far ahead of her. But when she rounded the next point, she found that the guy had pulled over as well, so there they were, together again. The frickin' lake's not that small, she shouted, apparently to herself; if he'd gone to the other side, she wouldn't've been able to smell him. No sooner had she paddled past him than he started up his motor again and putt-putt-putt-putt-putt-putt-putt-putted behind her. For half a frickin' hour.

But the worst, and this was door number three, was when the

guy had a radio in his boat. Turned up loud, so he could hear it. Because, after all, he was sitting right next to a two-stroke motor. And because he was hard of hearing. Because he spent so much time sitting right next to a two-stroke motor.

Which meant, of course, that everyone on the lake could hear the radio too.

I love you, baby, come to me, I love you baby, come to me [whimper], I want you baby, come to me, I want you baby, come to me [moan], You're all I need, don't you see that, you're all, you're everything [sigh], I love you, baby, come to me, I love you baby, come to me [whimper], I want you baby, come to me, I want you baby, come to me [moan], You're all I need, don't you see that, you're all, you're everything [sigh], Why do you treat me this way, oh baby [gasp] love you, baby, love you, what's your name again?

COME IN TODAY AND GET 30% OFF ALL DINING ROOM SETS, ALL COUCHES, ALL RECLINER CHAIRS, ALL KITCHEN SETS, YOU WON'T BELIEVE THE DEALS YOU CAN GET, BUT ONLY IF YOU HURRY, YOU HAVE TO COME IN NOW, THE SALE ENDS TODAY!! BUYING ONE OF OUR END TABLES WILL CHANGE YOUR LIFE FOREVER!!!!

Do you have unsightly stains on your teeth? Let us whiten your smile, brighten your life. At Dillen Dental, we take care of all your dental needs. O'Connor Drive, just past the overpass. Smile! You're at Dillen Dental!

IT'S GOING TO GET UP TO EIGHTEEN DEGREES TODAY, EIGHTEEN!!! Sunny with a bit of cloud moving in during the afternoon, but another BEAUTIFUL, BEAUTIFUL DAY!!

If you need a new car, don't forget to come down to Laney's Car Lot, where you'll find a lotta cars! We're getting rid of inventory to make way for a new shipment, so you won't believe the deals you'll find at Laney's Car Lot, where you'll find a lotta cars!

Let's get with the party, party, party, Let's get with it with the party, party, party, I'm walkin' with my baby, baby, baby, We're goin' to the party, party, party, She's so sexy, sexy, sexy, My baby is so sexy, sexy, sexy...

Yeah that's exactly what she wanted to listen to for two hours when she paddled out on a lake in a forest—

And the thing is, it became worse when the guy across the lake started holding his annual fishing derby. Because that put Paradise Lake on the map. And since there were a couple unofficial public access points, suddenly the lake was often full of people she didn't know. People who didn't know her. People who didn't know that if they came really close to her with their cigarette smoke and their inane conversation and their engine noise and their engine fumes and their radios, she'd just thwack them in the head with her paddle.

Speaking of the fishing derby, one weekend near the end of the summer, someone prepared an information sheet and left a pile at all the local bait shops:

Did you know that jetslams are bad news for us?
Not only does the noise scare the fish away,
which every fisherman knows,
but for every hour of operation,
a jetslam pours two gallons
of uncombusted fuel into the lake.

Two gallons of gas straight into the lake every hour.

There is a direct relationship between
the toxicity of the water and the size of fish.
A year from now, your fish could be this size:

And not even Viagra will make your little fish big again.

Apparently a fight broke out at the beer store between the jetslammers and the fishermen. When all was said and done—well, when all was done, since no one used their words—twenty-six guys were dead.

TurboJetslams

The fall was relatively good. There was the occasional afternoon, or morning, of chainsawing. Once or twice Tim and Lyle did something with their backhoe for a couple hours. But otherwise, it was pretty quiet.

Vic had been bracing herself for another three months of noise during which the Millers landscaped the devastated chunk of forest where the trenches for the geothermal pipes had gone. She'd thought they'd smooth it all out, then plant grass to make a yard. But nothing. Maybe they liked it the way it was: piles of uneven dirt, with broken rootlets sticking up all over the place. Maybe they were hoping it would grow over. Or maybe Jim was truly lazy after all. (Janet at least *walked* down to the water.)

That was a good thing of course. She'd heard them cut what little grass they had only once. And they did *nothing* down on the peninsula. *Nada.*

So she was feeling pretty good one night in early September, paddling back in the dark, no one on the lake but her and the beavers. It was so quiet, she could even hear their churring, a sort of snorting-with-your-mouth-full.

Then she rounded the last corner and was damn near blinded by a car heading straight toward her with its high beams on.

No—wait—that can't be, she was in the water. So what the—

Twenty minutes later, paddling with her eyes averted, she

was close enough to realize that someone had put a pair of those new super bright dock lights on the side of their dock.

Why in god's name do they need to light up the *side* of their dock? Have the jetslammers started going out at night? If so, she thought, the lights will probably just attract them.

As she paddled past, she saw that they had them on the front as well, *and* on the other side. Which meant they'd glare at her not only as she paddled back in the dark, but also when she was down on her dockraft. In the dark. The would-be dark.

On her break that night, she grabbed her screwdriver and walked over—because of course they weren't there, they were back in the city sound asleep—and unscrewed the lights on both sides, taking them home with her.

It was just easier that way.

Because, as was the case with so many other things—the water slide, the blow-up raft, the paddle boat, the pontoon boat, probably even the jetslams—they didn't 'want' dock lights until they saw them at the cottage show. Or in *Life at the Cottage*.

She saw that they'd also acquired a mini-lighthouse that flashed red, blue, and white. Thank god she wouldn't be able to see *that* from her place.

The woman across the lake with the runway lights would though.

So she left it there.

TurboJetslams

The rest of the month was relatively good. Except for the weekends, of course. Every one of the Sinclair teen-aged boys had a dirt bike. Two-stroke, without mufflers, like the ones Lyle and Tim had.

Fortunately, since they were teen-aged, they were allowed to go into the forest, instead of only up and down the lane.

Unfortunately, since they were stupid, they pretty much stuck to the logging road that went past Frankie's, never actually getting more than three miles away, never actually getting out of earshot.

One Saturday, when it was too windy to kayak, Vic started to head for the tent she'd pitched five miles into the bush, beside the second little lake. She'd been carrying things in bit by bit and now had in the tent a little portable propane single-burner, a mug, a gallon of water, and a stash of tea bags; a spare pair of reading glasses, several books, two pens, and a pad of paper; and one of those roll-up portable chairs people take to fireworks when they're too lazy to stand for fifteen minutes.

She stopped at the entrance at the bottom of the hill. Shit. Deer season had started that day. Anyone in the forest during deer season was liable to be accidentally shot. She was liable to be intentionally shot.

Then she heard the Sinclairs' dirt bikes revving up. They wouldn't know about deer season. And, like Bullert's crew, they took great delight in annoying people.

She waited until the first one rounded the corner, so he could see her step into the bush. Sure enough, when she was a mere twenty feet in, she heard him roar in behind her. She picked up Shiggles and jumped out of the way in time, then waited until all three—no—invariably, Dane got so focused on revving his engine, he didn't notice right away when, that, the others had left—four went in.

Only one came out.

Speaking of deer season, it pissed her off that she couldn't go into the forest during the best time of year. She seldom got to see the autumn colors—the deep burgundies, the bright reds, the scarlets and oranges, the brilliant golds—because she didn't want to get shot. Whose bright idea was it to allow men to hunt on *all* crown land?

And, she wondered, if this is such a *recreational* area—oh, right. Men consider killing to be recreation.

Even when it wasn't deer season, or moose season, or whatever-the-fuck season, there was a guy who set traps for wolves, just off the trails. Two of Shiggles' friends had already gotten caught in them. Fortunately she was with them both times. Nutter just got his leg caught and Beast was smart enough to sit perfectly still until she got to him and loosened the snare around his neck.

In fact, she loosened it so much, she pulled the wire right back through the catch.

Then did that for every trap she found.

Thereafter.

Another problem with the fall was that it brought windy weather. Windy weather in a forest meant trees went down. Windy weather in a forest where the hydro lines are strung from pole to pole meant the power went out.

Thirty seconds after the power went out, everyone's back-up generator went on.

Thirty-five seconds after the power went out, Vic's earplugs went in.

It's pathetic, she thought, that people, people who live in a forest, on a lake, can't do without their tvs for a couple hours. Or their vacuum cleaners. Or their power drills. Or whatever the hell it is they need their generators for.

Two hours after the power went out, they were on their way into town. Because 'What about supper?' What? Food is that foremost on your mind? This isn't Ethiopia. You ate just a couple hours ago. And if you're really that hungry, don't you have *anything* in the house that can be eaten raw or out of the can?

Or maybe they were driving into town because they couldn't stand the silence. No, that can't be right, she thought, because everyone's generator was going. There was no silence.

(Oh. So maybe they were driving into town because they couldn't stand their generator's noise. THEN TURN IT THE FUCK OFF!)

Is it that they couldn't stand the severance from—what, exactly? Society? Other people? Please. Most people here couldn't care less about other people.

Quite apart from the fact that a power outage doesn't sever you from society. Can't you hear everyone's generator? Everyone's still here, you're not alone.

Is it that people are so fearful, she wondered, that they need the illusion of safety that lights and noise and television—which has both light and noise, come to think of it—provides? Perhaps. Well over half of the people who lived on the lake year round never left their houses, she'd noted, except to get into their cars and go somewhere. She'd never seen them out for a walk, she'd never seen them down at the water, she'd never seen them out on the lake.

She hated that it was she who suffered the consequences of other people's fear.

And that she couldn't sabotage people's generators without losing her hearing.

Wait a minute—

She grabbed her earplugs, headphones, and iPod, put a few tools in the pocket of her jacket, called Shiggles, and headed out. She walked around to the other side of the lake. First driveway. No car. Okay, good. She picked up a few small rocks and started throwing. The power switch had to be—bingo! She walked right up to the generator, snipped a few wires, then strolled away.

Then strolled back to bury the evidence Shiggles had left.

Second driveway…

Understandably, she was beginning to love winters in her cabin on a lake in the forest. No backhoes. No dirt bikes. No ATVs. No jetslams. No screaming kids.

It would have been perfect. It would have been paradise.

Except that in the third week of December, Bullert and his buddies showed up in their pick-ups pulling trailers full of—snowmobiles.

The Sinclairs came up with their snowmobiles the week after.

Oh well, Vic thought, not to worry, there was a network of snowmobile trails available for their exclusive use. That's right. Ontario had kindly set aside 26,000 miles of trails just for snowmobilers.

Snowmobilers are a minority, she thought, angrily, when she had found out about this. Local business owners, who, she was told, benefit from snowmobilers, are also a minority. So why do they get to determine policy and practice? Policy and practice that affect other people? When they use their trails, no one else can. It's too damn unsafe. Ask my neighbour's cross-country ski friend, she muttered to herself. No, wait, you can't. She's dead.

And she wasn't even *on* the snowmobile trail. She was on the logging road they use to get to the trail.

Or, rather, the racetrack. Since that's what they used the trails for. Which meant our government had handed over thousands of miles of crown land to a bunch of men (yes, of course, they're almost all men) (well, boys) to use as their personal racetrack.

It would have been bad enough if they'd stayed on the trails. Even the non-designated trails.

But they also used the roads.

It's nice that we can hear a snowmobile coming from miles away, she'd thought to herself one day. While out walking on said roads. It means we have time to get out of their way.

But it wasn't enough, she'd discovered, to get off to the side (assuming that's not where you already were), because that was where the snowmobiles drove.

It wasn't even enough to get completely off the road and up onto the snowbank, because they liked to ride the banks.

You had to climb up *and over* the snowbanks to be safe.

No wonder the elderly couple had stopped walking in the winter.

In some countries, pedestrians had the right of way. In Canada, gas-guzzling, fume-spewing, noise-farting, male-driven snowmobiles did.

And *of course* they used the lake.

They zoomed up and down and up and down, and around, and around, and around, and up and down. They had to leave their tracks on every inch of the lake.

Which was breath-takingly beautiful before they'd arrived.

So she left a note on the Sinclairs' door after the first weekend, explaining how she so loved the pure white snow in front of her place, would they mind, when they were out snowmobiling, just turning around a few seconds earlier, *before* they got to her place? They had to turn around anyway, since she was at the end of the cove. It was a dead end. And she'd have to wait until the next snowfall for their criss-crossing tracks to get covered up. She thought maybe if the Sinclairs started turning around a couple lots before the end of the cove, Bullert and his buddies would follow suit.

What they started doing instead was making a point of coming into the cove, right to the end, right in front of her place, then tearing around for a good five minutes before heading back out onto the lake.

And, when she was out walking the following weekend, two snowmobiles roared to a stop a few feet from her. The guy on the first one got off, flipped up his helmet visor, and stomped over to her, his face black with rage. He started yelling at her and jabbing his finger at the air in front of her face.

"If you ever trespass on my property again, I'll sue!"

Trespass? Oh. She guessed she was trespassing when she left the note on his door. Geez. Get a grip.

And again she asked herself, how foolish is it to piss off those of us who are here 24/7, when you're not?

The weekend after that, the Sinclairs arrived to discover that a bunch of grouse had flown into their windows, breaking every one of them. Strange thing that. Middle of winter and all.

Then one Thursday in mid-February, after two months of this winter wonderland, and after a really good snowfall, Vic went out onto the lake with her shovel and built a ramp. Basically, she just moved the snow from here to there. 'There' being pretty much in front of the deranged beaver's dam. You know how spiders on LSD weave fucked-up webs? Half the anchor lines are hanging in mid-air and most of the radiating lines don't? There was a beaver on Paradise Lake that must've been similarly brain-damaged. She thought maybe it was because of all that gas in the lake. Anyway, it had built this bat-shit dam. Some of the trees it felled ended up being too big to drag. So they were just there in a jumble of pick-up-sticks-for-giants. Others were the right size, but once they were felled, they were used for abstract art, not a safe, secure home. So behind the jumble was a zig-zag palisade of pointy stumps. Thin, pointy stumps.

Friday afternoon, four o'clock, the Sinclairs and Bullert's crew arrived en masse. As soon as they turned off their pick-ups, they turned on their snowmobiles. As usual.

An hour later, they got on them.

And an hour after that, they saw the ramp. And couldn't resist.

The first one went over. His machine made a weird noise, then stopped.

The second guy didn't hear that because he was busy revving his machine. He went over. Probably landed on the first guy.

The third and fourth guys fought about who went over next. They went over together. Sweet.

The fifth guy was so pissed off to be last, his machine positively skyrocketed over the ramp.

None of them got up and walked away.

It was the quietest weekend they'd had in a very long time.

So why didn't she move? It was a reasonable question.

But where to? Although the place she'd rented on Manitoulin Island was relatively quiet—it was, after all, on a dead-end road set high on the cliff overlooking Gore Bay, and there was farmland on both sides—every day for an hour, three or four ATVs raced up and down the road. They probably thought that since it *was* a dead-end road, there wouldn't be any other traffic to watch for. Or patrol cars.

(The day before she left, someone let the cows out.)

(And all three, or four, ATVers went over the edge, in a truly stunning fashion, trying to avoid said cows. None of which, she was happy to say, were injured.)

(But there'd be another bunch of ATVers the next day, or the next week…)

She'd also rented a place on the Bruce Peninsula for a week, again to escape—something. (The generator across the lake when it was on 24/7?) But there too, there were jetslams. On the Bruce Trail side, not the Sauble Beach side. All those backpackers in their hiking boots, spending weeks in the forest with just their tents, their sleeping bags, and their trail mix, making their way along the trail on top of the cliff, overlooking the amazingly turquoise and teal water—they must have *loved* the jetslams zooming back and forth all day.

What should have happened, she thought, or should still happen, is some basic centralized planning. There were 250,000 lakes in Ontario. Why couldn't a third of them be designated for party animals of all breeds: they could race around on their vroom vrooms, get drunk, holler, get drunk, play their radios at full blast, get drunk... Another third could be designated for family fun: the kids could scream all day and not bother anyone, and it could be safe enough for them to swim without getting killed by a drunk, or sober, jetslammer. And the other third could be set aside for those wanting the peace and quiet, the beauty, the loons, the moonlight on the water. Rentals could be allowed at all lakes, but with restrictions according to their designation.

Failing that, she thought, there was no reason time zones couldn't be established on lakes too small for everyone to be out at the same time. The fishing boats could get the morning, the kids could get the mid-day, the jetslammers the afternoon, and the paddlers the evening.

But, she sighed, that would never happen.

What did happen was that over the course of a single year, gas prices "for non-essential use" went up from $1.50 a litre to $3.00 to $6.00 to $10.00. (A public education program followed about the meaning of 'essential'.) Finally, people in power had paid attention to Schumacher, Waring, Daly, and all the other no-growth pro-development steady-state economists who said it's quality that matters, not quantity, ya dickheads, who said we should put a price on the natural resources themselves, not just the labor men add to them, because it's *not* all about you, ya dickheads...)

The Levines, the Taylors, and a few other seasonals sold. The weekly trip to and from the city was more than they could afford even if they stopped fueling their toys, which was, so apparently, the raison d'être for the trip.

The trailer was abandoned.

The rental went unrented.

The only remaining (male) Sinclair was tinkering with their gas generator one night when power had gone out. He was smoking at the time. Turns out that what with John, Billy, Bobby, Bill, Jim, Junior, Ed, Riley, and Dane, there were over twenty jerry cans full of gas within fifty feet.

And then there were none.

Bullert landed in jail after he drove his snowmobile all over one of the local ski hills, screaming "You don't own the fucking mountain!" Don't quite know what he was convicted of. Could be a number of things. Manslaughter, for sure. Eighty-seven people died in the avalanche he caused.

Then both of the Millers lost their jobs. (Vic never did know what Janet did.) Turned out they didn't actually own any of their shit. They had to sell—everything. The aluminum boat, the canoe, the waterski boat, the paddle boat, what was left of the plane—the house. The property. All of it.

And they had to sell ASAP.

So the asking price was a mere $99,999.

What can she say, the price was right.

Turned out, though, she couldn't sever.

So she decided to rent.

While she looked for the perfect tenant, she got rid of the aluminum boat, the canoe, the waterski boat, the paddle boat, what was left of the plane, and the dock, the gazebo, the raft, and the other dock. Then she hired a landscaper to build up the land bridge between the hill and the peninsula, essentially creating a berm and a base for a dozen five-year-old already-five-feet tall trees.

Five months later, she found the perfect tenant. A deaf, mute quadriplegic. With no friends or relatives.

www.ingramcontent.com/pod-product-compliance
Ingram Content Group UK Ltd.
Pitfield, Milton Keynes, MK11 3LW, UK
UKHW041822200726
13854UKWH00002BA/506

9 781926 891651